"Why are you hovering outside my barn?"

Being alone with him was not good for her. If she kept busy and focused, he would stay out of her mind.

"Your niece was just telling me she needs a diaper change," he called from inside as if he could see her. "What is that aunt of yours doing, Jessie girl?"

Teeth clenched, Lexy stepped out of the bright light of the Texas sun into the cool shadows of his barn. Blinking, she paused to let her eyes adjust. She wasn't sure where he was. "Why do you have my niece?"

Jess squealed and kicked her legs in excitement. The colorful toys on the tray clattered and spun as the baby reached for Lexy.

Damian leaned over a half door, a currycomb in hand. He smiled—a real smile that changed his whole face. Were her eyes still not working?

He had dimples and creases that highlighted his eyes. The kind of lines that came from being outdoors. For a moment she forgot how to breathe.

A seventh-generation Texan, **Jolene Navarro** fills her life with family, faith and life's beautiful messiness. She knows that as much as the world changes, people stay the same: vow-keepers and heartbreakers. Jolene married a vow-keeper who shows her holding hands never gets old. When not writing, Jolene teaches art to inner-city teens and hangs out with her own four almost-grown kids. Find Jolene on Facebook or her blog, jolenenavarrowriter.com.

Books by Jolene Navarro

Love Inspired

Cowboys of Diamondback Ranch

The Texan's Secret Daughter
The Texan's Surprise Return
The Texan's Promise
The Texan's Unexpected Holiday

Lone Star Legacy

Texas Daddy
The Texan's Twins
Lone Star Christmas

Lone Star Holiday
Lone Star Hero
A Texas Christmas Wish
The Soldier's Surprise Family

Love Inspired Historical

Lone Star Bride

Visit the Author Profile page at Harlequin.com for more titles.

The Texan's Unexpected Holiday

Jolene Navarro

LOVE INSPIRED
INSPIRATIONAL ROMANCE

LOVE INSPIRED®
INSPIRATIONAL ROMANCE

Recycling programs for this product may not exist in your area.

ISBN-13: 978-1-335-48857-2

The Texan's Unexpected Holiday

Copyright © 2020 by Jolene Navarro

This edition published by arrangement with Harlequin Books S.A.

For questions and comments about the quality of this book, please contact us at CustomerService@Harlequin.com.

Love Inspired
22 Adelaide St. West, 40th Floor
Toronto, Ontario M5H 4E3, Canada
www.Harlequin.com

Printed in U.S.A.

For we walk by faith, not by sight:
We are confident, I say, and willing rather to be
absent from the body, and to be present with
the Lord. Wherefore we labour, that, whether
present or absent, we may be accepted of him.
For we must all appear before the judgment seat
of Christ; that every one may receive the things
done in his body, according to that he hath done,
whether it be good or bad.
—*2 Corinthians* 5:7–10

In memory of Dale Rumsey.
A man who made us feel welcomed into his
family the first time we hung out on the beach.
There was never a moment of awkward silence.
He reached out to those in need, going out of
his way to connect with people. But most of all
I remember seeing the love he had for his wife
and three children shine bright in his eyes.
You will be missed, and it is an honor
to accept your daughter into our family.

Acknowledgments

The writing is done alone,
but there is so much support and help along
the way to the end of the story. Thanks go to
Ani Jacob and Diane Morris of SARA
for sharing their scuba diving experience.

To my agent, Pam Hopkins,
for always being in my corner.

To my editor, Emily Rodmell, for helping me
find the perfect heroine for Damian.

To Fred Navarro for taking such good care of me
pre- and post-operation.
I couldn't do it without you.

Chapter One

Somewhere in the vast darkness, a cow lowed. Lexy Zapata stepped carefully through the strange terrain and shifted her eight-month-old niece to her other hip. Her sister followed as they made their way to the softly lit barn fifty yards off the road. They were somewhere close to the Texas coast. Or, at least, she hoped they were.

They'd been making their way to the Diamondback Ranch, and now Lexy wasn't sure if it was around the curve or still miles away. Apparently backcountry ranch roads were not on GPS

Baby Jess gripped Lexy's nose and laughed. Happy to be free of her car seat, her niece was wide awake.

The clouds danced around the full moon.

Moooo. Another cow answered the first.

Pressing her lips against Baby Jess's soft curls, Lexy sings "And the cow jumped over the moon."

"All we need is a little dog laughing to see the sight we're making," her sister, Naomi, said, somewhere from behind her. "This would have been so much simpler if the stupid gate would open."

The moon vanished behind the thick clouds. "I can't believe we're sneaking into a stranger's barn at two in the morning." The baby fussed against Lexy's shoulder "Shh. I'm right here, Jessie."

There was a thunk followed by a gasp.

"Naomi?" Lexy squinted into the dark, back down the overgrown dirt path. "Are you okay? Where are you?"

The tall form of her sister stood still on the other side of the cattle guard.

Behind her, the efficient compact car looked out of place parked on the other side of the barbed wire fence. It was pretty much useless now that the tank was almost empty. It had been over an hour since they had seen any real evidence of civilization.

With the car out of gas, a fussy baby and none of em having a clue where they were, Lexy had started aying. That's when she had spotted the barn.

Now getting to the barn had become a challenge. rossing the bars of a cattle guard freaked her sister ut, so Lexy had volunteered to carry the baby.

Another thud and an odd metal clanking sound filled he night air. "Sunday morning biscuits," Naomi grumbled.

Hearing her sister's quirky exclamation, she knew all was good. "Naomi? Did you fall between the bars and get sucked into the abyss?"

"I'm fine. I made it across that death trap, but I ran into a post and knocked off a bucket." She grabbed Lexy's arm, and they moved toward the barn together. "We'd never make it as cat burglars."

"I thought I knew what country was," Lexy said,

"but this is a whole new type of wide-open space. GPS can't even find us."

"This city girl needs street signs," Naomi complained. "There's nothing out here but miles of dirt roads and cows."

Lexy agreed. This was a whole other world from the street she lived on in Houston. In just fourteen hours, her life had completely changed. Naomi had called her in tears. Her little sister never cried, no matter how bad things got. She was made up of sunshine, puppies and butterflies. Ten years older, Lexy had been as much a mother to Naomi as a sister.

Whenever she had asked about the baby or how college was going, she got the happy smiling Naomi saying everything was great and she loved living in Dallas and school was awesome.

So she'd believed her. After years of taking care of her sick mother and little sister, Lexy spent the last two devoted to her career. Her love for scuba diving, environmental studies photography and writing were all coming together. But she had let her sister down because she had been selfish.

She had been relieved when Naomi had told her Steve was out of their lives. Then yesterday, Naomi called, and all his drama was back. Two men showed up at her door threatening her if she didn't turn over her boyfriend, Steve, or "the goods." They didn't believe her when she told them she didn't know where he lived anymore.

"I guess the good news," Naomi interrupted her thoughts, "is that Steve can't find us if we don't know where we are at."

Lexy bit back her frustration. Why had her sister told her sooner that Steve was dangerous?

After they left Steve showed up and accused her of stealing from him. He tore the place up, with a threat that he'd be back in the morning and he needed his bags.

Scared and with no idea what to do, she'd called Lexy. And for the first time was honest about her relationship with Steve.

Lexy wasn't letting her sister out of her sight again until they had the mess with Steven Hutchins cleaned up. Naomi and Jess would just have to stay with her until it was safe. She was moving anyway; Steve would have no way of finding Naomi if Lexy took her with her. So, she'd called her new boss and made arrangements to come a few days early.

And now they were here. Wherever *here* was.

Lexy stumbled over a rut in the pasture. She managed to keep hold of Jess, but the bag she was carrying hit the ground.

Naomi stooped to pick it up. "Lexy, I'm so sorry." It was probably the hundredth time she'd said it since they'd left Houston.

"It's okay, Naomi. We wouldn't be sneaking around in the middle of the night if I'd followed my instincts. If I'd made the time to visit you and Jess, we would have avoided all this."

"No. I'm nineteen now and should be making better choices. You've got your dream job and the chance to build this awesome life you've spent years planning. You put everything on hold for us for so long. It was your turn to go and…" There was a heavy pause. "I'm just sorry. You have to be tired of taking care of me."

"You're my baby sister. I love you. We're in this together. Seriously, stop apologizing." Lexy soothed her eight-month-old niece.

Not being able to handle the stress, Naomi's father had left them. All they had was each other. She had promised their mother she'd look after Naomi. Her little sister had been only six when their mother had been diagnosed with cancer. She had lived much longer than the doctors had predicted—almost eleven years—but that didn't make it any easier when they'd said goodbye.

Now it was just the two of them. *Well*. She smiled at the baby in her arms. *Three*. This precious little girl was named after their mother.

They crept up to the well-cared-for barn. It looked like something out of a top equestrian magazine. A little cabin stood nearby, probably the caretaker's quarters. "Look," Lexy said, pointing. "Maybe we should knock on the cabin door and asked for help."

"At two o'clock in the morning?" Her sister snorted. "Out here we might be shot first. And I'm not up to facing more angry men. I hit my limit already. We'll just sneak into the nice warm barn and, when the sun's up, we'll figure out where we are."

They found a door at the back of the barn, and Naomi slid it open. A single light came on. They both froze. Several horses turned to study them. A couple of them tossed their heads and made soft rumbling noises.

There was a comforting warmth inside the building. Lexy had always loved horses, and these seemed to be welcoming them home. A half wall to her left sectioned off a large space filled with bales of hay and bags of wood pellets. The place was clean and neat. She breathed in the calming scents of alfalfa, pine and leather.

"We can put the blanket down here and let Jessie stretch out." Naomi handed her the diaper bag, then strode to a corner and flung out the quilt. "I'm going to look around." As Lexy settled the baby on the blanket, Naomi walked toward the horses on the other side of the barn. With a gasp, she vanished through a door that was next to what looked like a large wash area for horses.

With a huge grin, she poked her head out. "This tack room has a full bathroom with a shower and it's clean." She practically skipped across the aisle. "Hand me my bag. We can brush our teeth and wash our hair. We don't have to look like stowaways when we meet your boss tomorrow. If you watch Jess, I'll take a long, hot shower. Then you can take one." Not waiting for a response, she rushed back through the side door, leaving it open.

"I think your momma is a bit too happy about the idea of a shower." She stretched out next to Baby Jess on the blanket. Tight muscles that Lexy had never met before eased and relaxed. "Ahh. It's good to be out of the car. I'm not sure I want to move again."

She grinned as the baby turned and rolled, grabbing a colorful toy and putting it in her mouth, then handing it to Lexy. "Thank you. Such a sweet little lady."

She stroked the baby's face till slowly the little eyelids closed, then fluttered open again. "Stop fighting sleep, baby girl."

A noise came from the front of the barn. Lexy sat up. A dog stepped over the threshold. A large dog that could do a lot of damage. She picked up Jess and wrapped her jacket around her.

A long shadow fell over the dog. A tall dark male followed closely behind. He was reaching for the wall.

Coming out the door behind him was her sister with a shovel in her hand. She lifted it.

"Naomi!"

He turned and ducked just as Naomi swung. The shovel caught the side of his face. Losing his balance, he fell. A gun slid across the brick floor.

Lexy held up her hand and yelled for her sister to stop. The man's dog rushed to him and nosed his cheek. Another dog, even bigger, stood just outside the door and barked. *"Quédate."* His voice was crisp as he ordered the dog to stay.

With Jess snug in her arms, Lexy rushed to her sister, who was looking a little wild-eyed and ready to attack again. She held up her hand again to Naomi as she turned her gaze to the man. He was glaring at them.

"Sir. *Está bien?*" Lexy asked.

"I'm fine," he replied, in clear English.

In one motion he stood. His right hand went to his opposite shoulder, then down the short sleeve of his dark blue T-shirt. His left arm ended right below the elbow with a crisscross of scars. She stared at the missing arm for a moment before he turned, blocking his left side from her view.

Naomi stepped back. "I called the police," she yelled as she waved her phone at the man. "They'll be here any minute."

He eyed the shovel, then them. The big dog with the black face stood by his side. A red mark had appeared on the man's cheek. "Good. Did you report someone trespassing on my property?" His voice was deep and a little gravelly, as if it didn't get used often.

Both dogs whined. He patted the one next to him and

whispered something too low to hear. "Hansel, *vienes.*" The dog in the doorway ran to his side.

A half sob came out of Naomi's throat. "If this is your barn, why are you sneaking around in the dark with a gun?"

All three adults shifted their gazes to his rifle a few feet away.

"On the ranch, it's common to carry a gun. There's a reason it's called the Diamondback Ranch." He lifted his arms, his one hand spread wide to show her he didn't have another weapon.

"We're on the Diamondback Ranch?" Relief flooded Lexy's muscles that had been tight since she'd realized they were lost in the dark. They had made it. "We didn't mean to cause any trouble. We're lost."

One of the horses responded, but the man didn't say a word. As he moved to retrieve his gun, Naomi gasped. He stopped midaction.

Lexy rushed her next words. "It's been a really stressful couple of days and we're a bit edgy around guns."

"I'm sorry about the shovel. I'm not a violent person. I saw your gun, and I just panicked." Naomi edged past the man, then rushed to Lexy's side. "I'm sorry."

He stood still. His gaze darted between them. Outside, the wind picked up. The temperature was dropping. Slowly he reached for the wall behind him and flipped a switch. Lexy blinked against the brightness that flooded the area.

His focus zeroed in on her. His features were hard and unforgiving.

They were an unusual greenish-gray color, framed by coal-black lashes and dark skin. Haunting images of the sweeping Spanish moss that hung from the ancient oak trees in the bayou came to mind. Taking a step away from him, Lexy lifted her chin.

Mouth dry, she cleared her throat. "I work for Quinn Sinclair. We'll be living on the ranch."

Great. Damian De La Rosa clenched his teeth and shifted his weight, resisting the urge to flex his knee.

Why did people keep showing up on his family ranch? There seemed to be someone new every time he turned around since his cousin had married the biologist.

This new interloper might be afraid of him, but the determination to protect her little family burned in her obsidian eyes. A fierce warrior lived in that short but solid body. Tons of dark brown curls threatened to escape a messy bun.

He frowned. The light pullover she was wearing wouldn't do much to keep her warm, but at least she had combat boots.

Reluctantly, he turned to the younger woman, the one who had swung at him. Other than being almost a foot taller than the one who'd distracted him, the women looked alike.

He reached for his rifle, and the taller one waved the phone again as if to ward him off. He sighed. The reason he lived deep on the ranch was so he didn't have to deal with people or explain himself. "It's not safe to leave the gun on the floor. I'll go lock it up. Then we can decide where you belong and how to get you there. Okay?"

He looked back to the shorter one holding the baby. She seemed to be in charge of the trio. He stayed still, waiting for her agreement.

She kept her back to the wall and her gaze on him.

"You said this was your property? Are you a De La Rosa?"

"Damian."

The baby whimpered and reached for the taller woman. With great care, the woman took the baby and moved back to cuddle her. With a soft *woof*, Gretel left his side and stood in front of the child.

He looked back at the older woman, his eyebrows raised. She shrugged and nodded toward the rifle. Damian picked it up and released, then cleared the chamber. Slinging the strap over his shoulder, he slipped the cartridge into his pocket, then snapped his fingers and pointed to his foot.

"Gretel, *vienes*." Head down, she turned toward him. But instead of walking over, she sat, her amber eyes begging to stay. "Seriously?" She made a low whine. He raised his eyes to the shorter woman. "Name?" His voice was harsher than he intended.

"Sorry." She stepped forward, right hand out. "I'm Lexy Zapata. This is my sister, Naomi Hernandez, and my niece, Jessie."

She wasn't the mother. No rings on either of their hands.

"My car was running low on gas and we're a little lost," she continued. "And by a little, I mean we had no clue as to our location. We just needed a place to rest and regroup before heading out in the morning. It's a relief to discover this is the Diamondback Ranch."

"Just the three of you?" He glanced around for a husband or boyfriend. There was no reason for him to care if she was single or not.

The sisters exchanged a glance, then her focus returned to him. "I was supposed to come alone, but my sister needed a place to stay for a while, so I brought her with me." She paused. "I spoke with Quinn. It's not a problem, is it?"

He shrugged. "No clue." In the morning he'd deliver the little family to Belle and hopefully not see them again. "There's a couple of cots in the tack room." He turned to leave, but Gretel whined again. With a shake of his head, he sighed. "She wants to stay."

Mouth back in a tight line, she met his gaze. "Is she a German shepherd?"

"No. Belgian Malinois."

Lexy went to the dog and held out her hand before stroking her behind the ears. "She's a beautiful dog." Tail wagging and with what had to be a smile, the dog lifted her eyes to the sister. "I think she likes babies. She's safe, right?"

He tried not to be insulted. "She's well trained."

With the baby balanced on her hip, Naomi went to her haunches next to her. The big dog dropped to her belly, her eyes on the little one. The woman held her hand out, palm up. "I can tell you're a good girl." Her voice was sing-song. His dog was eating it up.

The short one, Lexy, smiled for the first time, then glanced at him. "Sorry, we get a little silly over animals." Her attention went back to her niece. "Puppy."

Instantly his dog flopped to her back in complete surrender, and the child filled the room with the sweetest baby giggle. The females seemed to have created an instant tribe right in the middle of his stables.

An odd sensation settled at his core. He took a breath, but there was no rush to exhale. Something unfamiliar shifted under his skin.

Taking a moment to analyze the experience, he surprised himself with the conclusion.

A feeling of calm and peace had invaded this space. He looked over his shoulder. Making sure there was a clear escape.

He took a step back. The sooner this little family made it to Belle, the better. If it weren't two in the morning, he'd call her to come get her visitors. Better yet, he should just take them and drop them off on her front porch, but that wasn't socially acceptable behavior.

Lexy stood. "She's a good dog."

With one look at his big dogs, most people assumed the worst, just like they did with him. He snapped his fingers at his side for his dogs to join him. Gretel gave a soft bark, as if promising to be on her best behavior. The poor girl never asked for anything.

He glanced at his midnight trespasser. "Is it okay if she stays?"

She nodded. "That would be lovely."

"There are extra blankets in the cabin. I'll get them. Belle and Quinn are just about ten minutes from here. We'll go in my truck in the morning. There's a tank at the big barn where we can get you gas."

"Thank you, Damian, for helping us." She lifted her hand gracefully and waited for him to take it.

The hand was small but strong, and he wrapped his much larger one around it. A warmth eased through his skin. "*De nada.* You're going to love Belle. Everyone does."

His throat hurt from overuse. Too many words. It was time to go, so why was he lingering?

He hadn't talked this much since he'd been an inquisitive kid and his father would backhand him for his questions. Asking questions led only to trouble.

With his rifle back on his shoulder, he made his way to the cabin. Hansel stayed close to him, slipping one questioning look back at Gretel.

"She'll be back with us in the morning, boy." Pulling his jacket closer to ward off the dropping temperature, he resisted the urge to rub his hands together.

His brain thought it was fun to pretend he still had a left hand and foot. In the cabin, he locked away the rifle and ammo, then gathered the extra blankets.

Hansel tilted his head. "Yeah. It's getting colder and our travelers need a warm place to sleep." He didn't like people being in his space. "Gretel will make sure they're safe."

Hansel flopped down in his bedding with a heavy exhale of air as if he didn't agree.

Sleep would be good, but he wasn't going to get any tonight.

Blankets in hand, Damian went to the door. Hansel was back up and at his side. They'd probably end up spending the night on the porch until it was time to take their night travelers to the big house.

There was no way he'd be going to bed knowing they were out there alone.

Why would two women with a baby be traveling so late? Something wasn't right, but it wasn't his problem. By the time the sun came up, Belle would have them and they'd be out of his life.

That was good. He would hand her off to Belle and go back to his life the way he liked it. Quiet.

Chapter Two

A noise tickled Lexy's ear. She snuggled deeper into the warm cocoon of blankets. The soft rumbling of a horse tried to pull her from the cozy nest. Something wasn't right.

Eyes wide open, she shot up.

A horse? She took in her surroundings. *Stables?* She shook her head as last night came back to her. She looked to her side and found her sister and niece still sound asleep. A soft glow was peeking in through the barn windows. She glanced at her phone. Dead.

It had to be very early. The big dog that had been sleeping between them now stood at alert. A loud banging sound came from the opposite end of the stables. Reluctantly she pushed aside the pile of blankets Damian had given her and slipped on her boots.

Staying low, she eased her way toward the ruckus going on at the end of the stalls. It seemed to be coming from outside. Reaching the edge of the large door, she stepped over several split boards lying on the ground.

Hunched over, Damian looked as if he were trying to make himself smaller. On the other side of the broken fence was a beautiful black horse. He stood with his long legs wide, his head down and his nostrils flared as if he had sprinted a mile. Blood dripped from one of his front legs.

Damian eased forward, hand out. "It's okay, boy. I'm not going to hurt you."

The horse threw his head and spun around, charging the metal panel behind him. Damian stepped back and held his right arm out. He pressed his back to the post behind him and blew out a large huff of air. His warm breath collided with the cold morning, creating a thick fog.

The horse and man were in a staring contest.

"Can I help?" She wasn't sure what she could do, but that horse was hurting, and she was never able to walk away from anyone that needed help. Even when they didn't want it. Which had gotten her in trouble more than once.

Damian broke eye contact with the angry horse and looked at her. "I wish. I have yet to come across an animal I couldn't work with. I think I've met my match. This is King's Ransom. He has a bit of an attitude."

"Did we upset him last night?"

"No. Maybe. He doesn't like being in small places. I thought the paddock would be open enough for him, but—" he gestured to the busted fence "—apparently, it's not enough room. He's going to get himself killed trying to make a run for the open pasture."

The horse kicked at the barrier behind him. Blood dripped from a new cut. He tossed his head and snorted. Lexy left the covering of the stables and stepped into the paddock area he had broken out of. "Hey, King. You're a beautiful boy."

The horse lunged and stomped his front hooves at her. She crouched a few feet behind Damian.

"Maybe you should go back inside," Damian said.

"Why not turn him loose in the pastures?"

"He's worth too much to turn loose. His owners don't want to risk any injuries."

She raised an eyebrow, then looked back at the horse. "His efforts to free himself are making a bloody mess of his legs and head."

With a sigh, he nodded. "Yeah. The agreement needs to be revisited." Making a small movement closer, he spoke to her but kept his gaze locked on the horse. "Keep talking. I think he likes your voice."

"Really? What do you want me to say?" The horse did seem to be calming down. His head hung low, and his ears twitched from her to Damian.

"Just talk."

"Hey diddle, diddle, the cat and the fiddle, the cow jumped over the moon. The little dog laughed to see such a sight and the charming dish ran away with the spoon."

The horse gave her his full attention. Damian snorted. "Really? I don't remember a charming dish."

"My own version. You wanted me to talk and I panicked. I was reciting it to Jess last night. Seemed appropriate with all the cows, the full moon and us sneaking around a strange place." She kept her voice even.

Damian had gotten within a couple of feet of the horse. King was ignoring him. With his palm flat, Damian reached out, offering a couple of green cubes. She nodded to his outstretched hand. "What are those?"

"Alfalfa treats." Snorting, the horse stepped farther

back and pawed the ground. He pushed his hindquarters against the stall wall, his ears flat.

Damian gave her a quick glance. "Know any other nursery rhymes?"

She started with "Rub-a-Dub-Dub," then moved on to other favorite childhood books. The parts she remembered, anyway. The horse's breathing slowed, and the whites of his eyes disappeared.

Not wanting to stop, she went for a story that could make her cry. She could probably recite it word for word in her sleep. The mother loved the child through all the ups and downs of childhood, even through the teen years when he thought he was too manly for a goodnight kiss. Then the boy grew up and he had to love his mother through her illness and death. By the end, he makes the same promise that she always made him, to love her forever and always.

As she finished, she glanced at Damian. His jaw was clenched, and his eyes glistened. Were they wet? The horse nosed another cube and took it from him. Damian rubbed the underside of the big jaw. "That's a good boy."

"Are you okay?" She wanted to reach out, but she resisted. Instead, she wrapped her arms around her waist. "That one gets to me every time."

"So why?" He took another cube from his pocket. Without looking at her, he moved along the horse's side.

"Umm. I'd run out of things to say. My mom used to read it to me. Then I read it to my sister every night. Now I read it to Jess over the phone. The words are burned into my brain. I'm sorry if it upset you."

"No. No. It surprised me. Hadn't heard it since I was little. It reminds me of my mom—she used to read it."

"It's a very sweet but sad story. With my mom getting so sick and dying, it means even more to me." She swallowed. "You've lost your mother?"

He ran a hand over the horse's wide forehead. "Yeah. But it was a long time ago."

"I'm sorry. Losing a mom is never easy." The horse was still listening to her. "The rhythm is soothing. I thought he needed to hear it."

Lexy watched as Damian bent down. Something was off with his left leg. Was it damaged or was it missing like his arm?

"Would you hand me the caddy by the wall?" He pointed to the left of her.

"Sure." Without any sudden movements, she went to the area and picked up the supplies. "The water too?"

"Yes. Hold them out so he can see them. Keep talking."

She wasn't sure what to talk about, so she described everything she carried. Not sure how close to get, she kept her steps small. Half of what she said was nonsense.

"That's good." Damian stopped her. The horse stretched his neck to sniff the bucket. He took a step forward and his soft muzzle brushed the back of her hand. Not sure what to do, she glanced at Damian.

"It's okay. He likes you." He grinned. "This is good. Hand me the washcloth and keep talking." He used it to wipe the banged-up areas as she talked about how beautiful King was. Standing, Damian handed her the wet rag. "Give me the one with the ointment."

"I don't know if I've ever talked this much nonstop in my life before."

"Join the club." His body stayed close to the powerful animal as he explained what he was doing and why.

Every movement was slow and steady. Power radiated from this man, but he was so gentle in everything he did. The contradiction fascinated her.

The sun made its way over the horizon. The soft glow of early morning light revealed the hidden red in the dark hair of both the man and the horse. It was so serene. She wished she had her camera. "You have the same color of hair."

Forehead pulled into a V, he looked at her as if she'd claimed to have seen a mermaid. Then he shook his head. "Open the gate?"

"Sure laddie, right as rain." She pressed her lips together to stop her bad Irish accent. That didn't even make sense. Why did she always do that when she was nervous?

He shot her a confused look over his shoulder.

Pretending she hadn't said anything weird, she ignored him. With slow measured her steps, she made it to the gate, then pushed the sliding bar. "Are you turning him out?"

"This pasture should be safe enough for now, and he's calmed down. Letting him out now reinforces good manners." Damian stepped back, making the path to the opening clear. King took a few tentative steps, then stopped at her.

Holding her breath, she waited. He lifted his muzzle to her and blew warm air into her face. She chuckled. "Yes. I like you too."

With a flick of his tail, he stepped through the gate. Once on the other side, he stood still for a moment. Then, in a burst of raw energy, he reared and lunged forward. The long, powerful legs stretched as he ran full out across the pasture. She held her breath at the beauty of his movements.

"What happened to him? Was he abused?"

"Not physically. At three months he was taken from his mother in California and on the trip to Texas there was an accident. He was the only one to survive, but they didn't find the truck and trailer for two days. He'd been trapped. He's three now and on his fourth owner."

She gasped and studied the magnificent creature now prancing along the outer fence, head high. "Do you train horses?"

"I work with them so they can deal with human expectations."

She frowned. Was he a horse therapist? Before she could ask, he was already in the barn.

When she caught up with him, he was standing at the door where Naomi and Jess were still sleeping. "We're late. In ten minutes, I'll have the truck running. Be ready." Then he was gone.

"Late?" She glanced at the sun still hugging the horizon away the darkness. They obviously had different ideas of what late meant.

His passengers groaned as they hit another pothole. He frowned. When had the roads become this bad? Lexy bounced against the door with each rut and hole. He slowed his truck and moved to the edge of the dirt road, trying to find a smoother path. Glancing in the rearview mirror, he checked on the backseat passengers.

With her chin on the edge of the car seat, Gretel was still glued to the baby. Naomi looked a sickly shade of green. He eased up on the gas. His truck wasn't built for pleasure cruises.

Hansel was between Damian and Lexy. The dog's glare made his mood clear. Hansel hated the company as much as he did. Gretel was much more social. At least the women were quiet.

"Does your head hurt from the shovel?" And the blissful silence was gone. They were the first words Lexy had spoken since he'd pulled up to the barn with his truck. He'd foolishly hoped she'd realized he liked silence. Especially with the throbbing at his temple, and in the back of his head, and behind his eyes. Yeah, his whole head hurt.

"Damian?"

"What?"

"Does it hurt?"

"No."

She crossed her arms and frowned. "Should you see a doctor? You could have a concussion. I should be driving."

"You don't know where you're at or where to go. I've had much worse. No doctor."

The drive between his cabin and the big house had never lasted so long. It seemed to take forever to go around the old barns and through the surrounding pastures.

A couple of cows stopped in the middle of the road and stared at them.

"I guess this is your idea of a traffic jam." Amusement lit up her face. "Is this all your ranch?"

He looked at it through new eyes. There were still so many repairs and additions he'd ignored. Most of it to spite his father, who was gone. It was Belle's now, and she worked hard to keep it going, but there was so much one person could do. She deserved more from him. "Belle's been running it alone for years."

"Belle! I'm excited to meet her. The whole foundation was so excited when we heard Quinn was marrying the ranch owner. What a story. How are you related to my boss's new wife?"

"She's my cousin, but my parents took her in when she was small, so she's more like a sister. When all the boys left, she stayed and helped hold the place together. She's the toughest of the De La Rosas. The daily operations of the ranch are all hers."

"You don't work on the ranch?"

He almost grinned. "Most would say I hide." Finally, the big house built by his grandfather came into view. For the longest time, he had refused to step foot through the door. It was the house that held his worst memories, but Belle lived there now and, room by room, she had swept the place clean of his father.

He parked in front of the porch but didn't cut his engine. "Quinn's here. Once Belle feeds you, I'm sure she'll find a room you can crash in until y'all figure out the details. If your keys are in the car, I can bring it to you."

"Oh, no. I'll go with you now that I know the roads."

She seemed to have missed the point that he wanted to be alone.

Belle charged through the door and down the steps. She went by Sinclair now, but to him she'd always be a De La Rosa. Her long dark hair hung in two braids over her shoulders. She was a tall woman who looked as if she'd stepped straight out of an old Western. Strong and independent didn't even start to describe her. She was the poster child for a Texas rancher. If his passengers didn't move faster, she'd trap him here for hours.

Quinn, her new husband, trailed right behind her. He looked more surfer dude than ranch cowboy. Damian had to smile. The marine biologist was perfect for Belle. Several children filed out the door. Belle's two daughters and Quinn's three kids had blended so smoothly it was hard to imagine them as separate units.

Naomi unbuckled the baby from her car seat, and Gretel jumped out as if making plans to stay too.

With a huge grin on her face, Belle waved. She was just steps away, and Lexy was still in the truck. His heart kicked up a pace. They were going to make him stay if he didn't do something fast. Belle turned and said something, and the small herd of girls and one boy disappeared back into the house.

"That's Belle. You know her husband, Quinn, and that flock of kids are all theirs. They're more harmless than they look, I promise. Go ahead and get out. They'll take care of you." *Hurry*, he wanted to yell, but that seemed rude, even for him.

Belle opened his door. He sighed in defeat. The plan to drop them off and run had failed. He might as well help with the bags.

As soon as his boots hit the ground, Belle hugged him. She was good at ignoring his protests. Quinn patted him on the back, then turned to greet Lexy.

"Oh, Quinn." Belle took Jess. "Look at this baby girl. She's too precious."

As Lexy introduced herself and Naomi, Damian took the bags to the porch. Everyone made noises over the baby, even Quinn. It was a good time to slip back into his truck and leave.

But Belle cut him off. "Where do you think you're going? You're not leaving until I feed you." Her brows wrinkled. "And explain that bruise on your face. Is it the new horse?"

"No. It was just me being careless." He didn't look at either of the women who knew the truth. "I can't stay. The new horse from Vaccaro's place needs lots of work, and my schedule has been—"

"Nope." Belle cut him off. With a shake of her head and the baby tucked tight against her, Belle pointed to the house. "Everyone in. I have enough food to feed the whole De La Rosa crew, so you're not sneaking away yet. Xavier is on his way with Selena." She looked to Lexy. "They are Damian's brother and sister-in-law. I think Elijah, my brother, is coming too."

"Belle." His voice had a low warning in it. "Careful. The De La Rosa family in full force can be intimidating. I'm not sure if they're up for that hefty of a dose."

"It's fine. You can never have too much family or too many friends." Belle winked.

He could totally argue against that point, but it wasn't worth it. Hansel stayed right next to him as they made their way to the front porch.

Gretel walked between Belle and Naomi, her eyes on the baby.

Belle laughed. It was happening more often, thanks to Quinn. It was a sound Damian could never get enough of—not that he'd tell her that. She bumped him with her shoulder. "I'm thinking Gretel has abandoned you for a new person."

Lexy looked stricken. "Oh, no. She's Damian's dog."

"It's clear that Gretel has claimed your family, whether you agree or not. I've never seen her away from Damian's side since we brought her to the ranch. She was going to be euthanized. Hansel served with him in the Middle East." She patted the dog. "Damian saved them both. He's good at that. Talking to hurt animals is his super-power."

He grunted. "They're perfectly good dogs. Nothing wrong other than they're big and a bit rough looking. They just need work." He shrugged.

Inside the house, he closed the door behind him, and Belle led the way to a large country kitchen. The aroma of food made him grateful for Belle's stubbornness.

Okay, so he'd make sure Lexy and her sister were settled, get a quick bite, then get back to his place. Back to right his world that had been disturbed last night.

Lexy fought the urge to stare at Damian. One, it was rude, and two, she had no business being intrigued by a man she didn't know. Even though he was Quinn's in-law, he was a stranger—and one who didn't seem to want people around. She straightened her spine. "Anything I can do to help?"

"Sit. Sit. Sit." Belle smiled at her. She added bowls full of scrambled eggs and potatoes to the table.

Quinn pulled a pan of giant cinnamon rolls out of the oven and set them in the center of the dishes. As if that wasn't enough, Belle brought over a basket with something wrapped in a kitchen towel and a plate piled with bacon and sausage.

Lexy glanced at Naomi and found her sister looking as overwhelmed as she felt.

"I wasn't sure what you liked, so I tried a bit of every-thing." Belle sat next to Quinn. "The kids should be—"

Their children rushed in, going straight to the sink to

wash. It had been a year since she'd seen Quinn's kids and they had grown a few inches in that time.

Belle smiled. "And there they are. That's Cassie, my oldest. I think you know Quinn's twins, Meg and Hannah, and his son, Jonah." The smallest one in the group ran and hugged her, dark curls flying around her face. "This is Lucy."

Belle did a quick job of putting the child's loose strands back into her ponytail holder. "Sit down so we can pray."

All five kids scrambled to chairs and lowered their heads. Hands out, they made a circle. Lexy took Naomi's hand on her left and Quinn's on her right. Her boss led them in a blessing that almost had her in tears. How long had it been since she had taken the time to give thanks over a meal? When was the last time she'd sat at a family table in front of a meal prepared with love? Those little moments had slipped past, and she hadn't even realized they were gone until now.

This had been the norm growing up. Her mother had always made sure they had at least one meal at the table as a family. Prayers were a daily routine. When had she lost this?

She sent her own thanks to God. A minute passed as she realized the others had finished and were waiting for her. Heat crept up her neck. "Sorry."

"Don't be. Sometimes we just need that extra time. Y'all had a crazy day and night. I can't believe you slept in Damian's stable. Of course, he takes such good care of the horses, it's probably better than his cabin."

Damian grunted what could have been a scoff, but then reached for more breakfast. The simple action had the muscles in his shoulders flexing.

Lexy swung her gaze to Belle. "The stables were very comfortable. I've always loved the smell of being around horses. The hay, the leather, the pine. It's my second favorite." She bit her lip to stop talking. Why was she babbling?

The food was passed around. The kids made breakfast tacos. Her stomach rumbled. She didn't know where to start. "This is amazing. Thank you."

"What's your first?" Damian asked from across the table.

She blinked, surprised he had spoken. "My first?"

"You said the smells in the stable are your second favorite. What's your first?"

"Oh." She relaxed. "The ocean. Early morning on the beach. Fresh salt air. I live for that."

"You're in the perfect place, then." Quinn winked at her, then turned to the others. "Lexy is one of my best divers and you should see her photography. Stunning. Ocean is my favorite too."

"I love the smell of my mama's cinnamon rolls. It's why I get up in the morning." Jonah smiled as he took a big bite of the gooey goodness. The kids took turns telling their favorite aromas. Then the adults. Everyone but Damian.

Lexy couldn't resist. "What about you?" She'd tried to ignore him, but that hadn't lasted even thirty seconds. She wanted to know more about him.

"Alfalfa hay, leather and fresh shavings in the stalls. Second is the smell of the ocean after a storm."

He looked at her, the right side of his mouth in a slight curl. A connection zapped under her skin.

Nope. Nope. Nope. Not a connection. She had nothing in common with this man who hid in the middle of nowhere and liked living alone in a tiny cabin.

She loved people, going places, exploring the world. There was nothing connecting them.

Chapter Three

Damian moved to put his plate in the sink. Belle was in charge. Lexy would be well taken care of. She wasn't his responsibility anymore. With the family's attention elsewhere, Damian casually made his way to the front room. If he moved slowly enough, his attempted escape might go undetected by Belle.

Quinn leaned forward. "You'll be able to get some spectacular shots on the shoreline and underwater. I know you weren't supposed to report for another week, but if you want, Monday morning I can connect you to Hunter. He'll be running the program while Belle and I are out of the country. For now, Belle can get you settled here on the ranch."

"Are you sure it's okay?" She glanced at all the innocent faces around the table. "I don't want to bring any trouble to your door."

"We're the De La Rosa family. We know how to handle trouble. You and your sister are in the perfect place. I'm glad we could be here for you. I've been following your blog too. Nice work. Now, you get some much-needed rest, then we'll get you settled in one of the cabins."

Quinn stood and braced his hands on the back of his chair. "I know we had planned for you to be based here for a year, but I've got a couple of places outside the US where we need a diver and photographer. Getting your family out of the country might be a good option. One is in South America, the other in Australia." He looked at Naomi. "Do you have a passport?"

"No."

He nodded and looked back at Lexy. "Take care of that, and this next week you and I will talk in detail about the other jobs. I'll be back in a couple of hours." Quinn kissed his wife, then left out the back door.

Damian wanted to ask what trouble had her worried, but then he'd have their attention. The front room was one step away when Belle moved in front of him and smiled. He should have known better.

"Where are you going?"

He sighed. "I need to get back to work." He was going to have to make a run for it, but only Hansel was at his side.

With a motion of his hand, he called Gretel to him. She lay at the base of the high chair Jess was strapped into. Her ears were tucked back and her tail slowly thumped against the wood floor.

"Gretel. *Vienes.*" He snapped his fingers. She lifted herself off the floor, but she watched him with her head down.

"Really, Damian?" Belle sighed. "You'll be fine without her for a few days. Let her stay until they get comfortable." She glanced at Lexy. "Would that be all right with you?"

Approaching the table, Damian stood next to the baby. He put a hand on the dog's head and looked her in the eyes. Then he glanced at Lexy. Less than twenty-four hours and she had already unsettled his world. "She can stay with you if you want her to." He looked down at the dog. She was happy. Maybe she needed other people more than he thought. It was selfish of him to keep her isolated because that was what he wanted. He nodded. "She's happy with you. Is it okay?"

"Yes."

With a nod he went out the door, putting the new residents of Diamondback Ranch out of his mind.

Before leaping into the truck, Hansel gave the ranch house one last, long gaze, as if expecting Gretel to change her mind.

"I think she needs more than we can give her, boy." He patted the dog, then put his truck in gear and left. "It's fine. Everything that makes life good for us is at the cabin."

As he turned out of the drive, Xavier's Jeep came into view. Elijah was close behind. "Looks like we got out just in time." They waved, but he kept going.

His cabin and horses were waiting. That was all he wanted. A quiet place without another person in sight.

The natural light from the large windows washed the kitchen in welcoming warmth. Jess babbled on a blanket just a few feet away in the living room. Gretel was right next to her. She was surrounded by Belle and Quinn's kids as they watched a sing-along show.

Belle was at the sink, washing up from spending the day working outdoors. Naomi was resting in the guest room. "Please let me make dinner," Lexy said.

"You've been working all day and we're an unexpected intrusion."

"Nonsense. I'm always ready to feed people. I dreamed of having a home that was a safe harbor in a storm. Welcoming you and your sister gives me joy. And that precious baby fills my heart. You might be unexpected, but never an intrusion."

She brought a couple of bowls and a bag of pinto beans to the table. "That being said, I will accept any offer of help." She laughed as she poured the beans onto the table. "With all the kids and my family stopping in, I'm always running low on frijoles. Mind helping me get a new batch started? It will give me an opportunity to sit for a moment."

Lexy sat where she could still see Jess as she helped Belle sort the good beans from the bad and pull out a few random rocks.

They worked in silence while the sound of children filtered around them. Once the beans were seasoned in the slow cooker, Belle sat back. "Now we need to get down to business. I'm looking at our list of cabins available and it has me thinking you might also be able to help me with another need I have. You can say no and it's fine, but how do you feel about taking on an additional part-time job?"

"Extra money is always good. What is it?"

The other woman leaned in and crossed her arms. "Just running a few errands for Damian and checking in on him."

"Damian? Why does he need checking on?" Unease crept along her nerves.

"Not sure if you noticed, but he's extremely antisocial. Growing up, he was always a loner, but when he came back from the service it was worse. Of course, it was to be expected. At first, we let him withdraw. The loss of his arm and lower leg was a hard adjustment. I'm so proud of the work he's put in and I thought he was fully coming back to himself. But then Frank died, and he pretty much become a shut-in."

"Frank?"

"Damian and Xavier's father, my uncle. He also raised my brother and me. Damian found his father in the back four-fifty. He'd been dead for a while. Since then, Damian refuses to go into town or even interact with people online. I've given him room, but his behavior has gotten worse and I'm worried about him."

"I can't tell he's missing part of his leg."

"I know, but it wasn't easy." With a soft laugh, Belle grinned. "Sometimes the De La Rosas' stubbornness pays off. He's amazing and it hasn't stopped him from doing the things he loves. Working with his horses, mostly. But he's gotten downright grumpy and non-verbal the last year."

"Really? I mean, he seems quiet, but he was very nice. And he spoke plenty with me."

Belle hollered out a laugh, causing the kids to look at them. "See? No one else has ever said that about him. He's different around you. I noticed his rifle was missing. He hasn't been without that, ever."

"We asked that he not have it around the baby." Lexy focused on her hands, wishing she had something to do.

Belle gave her another strange look. Lexy didn't know her well, but she could tell there were plans, thoughts and ideas turning over, and they all included her and Damian. "Really, I'm not looking for any kind of relationship."

"Oh, I'm the last person to play matchmaker. It's just that most people are afraid of him and refuse to go out there unless I'm with them. Quinn and I are traveling out of the country Monday afternoon. I haven't left the ranch in years. We'll be back before Christmas and I would feel so relaxed if I knew someone had an eye out for Damian."

"But you don't even know me."

"Quinn said you did your college internship at the foundation headquarters in Houston while you were taking care of your mother and raising your little sister. He was so impressed with you that he hired you as soon as the internship was over."

"I didn't have much of a choice. Our mom was sick. Cancer. Then we lost her, and Naomi's decisions since have not been the best." Now she was getting too personal. "I'm sorry. I just want to keep my family together and safe."

"Believe me when I say I understand that as well as anyone can." Belle reached across and covered her hand with fingers that were gentle but roughened by ranch work. Lexy figured that pretty much summed Belle up.

"We lost Damian's mom to cancer. She raised me. The only mother I really had. It's hard, but you can't blame yourself."

"Damian's mom? He said he lost her when he was young, but he didn't say how."

"He told you that?" Belle shifted. Her eyes wide.

Unease tightened Lexy's skin. She had said too much. Belle was drawing all sorts of wrong conclusions.

With a small squeeze of her hand, Belle smiled and moved back. "Well, Quinn says you are hardworking, loyal and compassionate with a healthy streak of stubbornness. And most important? Damian likes you and so does Gretel."

Not knowing what to say, Lexy turned her attention to her niece and the new family guard dog.

"Anyway. I'm going south with Quinn for a couple of weeks, but I was nervous about leaving Damian. I need someone to check the mail, gather the eggs each day, and take deliveries out to Damian and look in on him."

"That doesn't sound like too much."

Belle sighed and sat back. "Delivering his mail allows me to do wellness checks to make sure he's eating and resting. There are complications that can happen on a lower limb if the prosthesis is overused. He's very active."

"Does he know you do all that?"

She twisted her mouth to the side and shook her head. "Not really. He knows I'm checking his refrigerator and that I deal with all his correspondence for his business. He rehabs horses and I respond to the emails he gets. He likes that I do that for him. It means he doesn't have to deal with people."

She stopped suddenly and blew out a puff of air.

"Wow. Damian. I'm making it worse." She rubbed her temples. "Because of me, he doesn't have to go anywhere or talk to anyone." She leaned back and crossed her arms. "I just had an epiphany. When I get back, I think I need to talk to a counselor. Because of the way we were raised, we're a bit overprotective of each other. It never occurred to me that I'm enabling him and making it worse."

"He seems fine—more than fine—on his own."

She sighed. "He is, but… I don't know. I need to think about this. Anyway, personal family drama aside.

I have an empty cabin next to his. I've never put any-one there because he would scare them off. But since I'm going to be traveling more, it would be nice to have someone out there with him. You'd have your own place, but not be completely isolated."

That brought a lot of questions to mind, but Lexy bit back the personal ones. "Why not Xavier or Elijah?" She'd just met them that morning, but the family seemed close. "Are there any more of you?"

"There's a total of four De La Rosas in town. My brother, Elijah and I were dropped off by our mom as little kids. Frank was our uncle, Xavier and Damian's dad. So, we were raised together. They have a younger sister, but we lost touch of her after their mom died. Da-mian and I are the only ones that actually live on the ranch. We grew up together and we look out for each other. My uncle wasn't a nice man, and I'm not sure if Damian's issues come from his service in the Middle East or the upbringing we had to survive." Belle leaned forward as if to share a secret, but a door opened in the front of the house.

The kids cheered. "Tío Damian!"

Belle raised an incredulous eyebrow at Lexy. "He's here?" She stood, but Damian was already in the door-way.

"I brought Lexy's car. I filled the tank." He held up a short chain with her sand dollar. "This was on the floorboard. It looked special and they break easily."

She gently took the precious piece from him. Emo-tion burned her throat. "Thank you." She blinked back tears at the thought of losing it. "My mom found it dur-ing our last walk on the beach."

For a moment they held eye contact, a softness lightened his gray eyes to green, but then it was gone. With a nod, he turned to leave.

"Damian." Belle stopped him. "How are you getting back?"

"Walking." His forehead pulled as if she had asked a ridiculous question.

"That's almost five miles with uneven terrain." Belle had her hands on her hips.

With a heavy sigh, he turned away. "I know where I live."

"Wait. We need your help."

He twisted his head to face her. "First you imply I'm unfit to walk to my place, then you suddenly need my help?"

"I've decided to move Lexy and Naomi to the cabin next to yours."

A heavy silence fell between them as he narrowed his gaze at Belle for a long second. "Why?"

"Originally it was just her, but with her sister and baby, they need more room. That's the largest cabin and it's close enough to you that if something happens, you're right there to help. Also, I'm going to be traveling more, so I've asked her to bring your supplies to you. It'll make it easier if she's close."

"I don't need a babysitter." He just about growled.

Belle rolled her eyes. "Maybe you do, but that's not why I'm moving her out there. Which cabin do you think I should put them in?"

Damian turned to her. "Are you okay with being that close to me?"

"I'm fine." Just because they were neighbors didn't mean she would have to spend time with him. "We'll be very quiet." Her Irish accent rolled off her tongue. She cleared her throat. "We won't bother you."

Belle's wide smile beamed at them. "Good. It's settled. Now can you help us move her?"

"Other than our few bags here, everything we have is in my car. We don't need much. Is there a washer and dryer? Naomi uses cloth diapers most of the time."

"There's a hookup. If we don't have them there, we can get them. Do you have everything else you need? I think the cabin is furnished with the basics, but it's been a while since I checked it. I have an extra crib you can use. I'm not sure of the condition it's in. We'll take a tub of cleaning supplies and groceries."

"I have money for food. I just need directions to town. Don't worry about the condition. I can clean it."

"I'm not going to just drop you off and let you fend for yourself. It's getting late and, since you don't know the area, let's stock your pantry. Then you can go into town when it's convenient. Thanksgiving is tomorrow. You should join us."

Naomi walked into the kitchen. She had picked up Jess. Gretel followed closely at her heels, her eyes focused on the baby. "Thanks for letting me get that extra sleep."

"No problem. Are you ready to see our new home?"

Naomi smiled and nodded. "Yes, we are." She kissed her daughter's forehead.

Belle clapped her hands. "Kids, come on, we're taking Ms. Lexy and Ms. Naomi to their new home. They're moving into the cabin next to Tío Damian."

Cassie, Belle's oldest jumped up, her eyes wide. "Really? Does Tío Damian know?"

Damian grabbed her in a headlock and kissed the top of her head. "Yes, brat."

The girl laughed as she twisted out of his grasp.

Lexy looked at Jessie's big eyes. "Are you ready for our new adventure?" Happiness settled in her heart. She had her family together and the best job ever.

A warm hand covered her shoulder, and Belle touched the baby's tiny fist. "Welcome to Diamondback Ranch."

Why did it feel as if she had arrived home? She had been so busy achieving her dreams since her mother's death she hadn't realized she missed this sense of belonging. Of being a part of a family.

But as welcoming as Belle and the ranch felt, she couldn't drop her guard. When she hadn't been watching a threat hit her sister and niece.

Now she had hold it together. She had to stay vigilant.

Chapter Four

His quiet little world had been invaded. Since last night, Damian had had more interaction with people than he'd had in the last two years. He longed to get back to the barn, to his safe place.

So why was he leaning on his truck, waiting, instead of getting in and leaving? The little cabin that had been shut up and abandoned for over five years was brimming with new life.

On the back porch, Lexy swept the last of the dirt and cobwebs off the steps. Her dark hair swung in a ponytail. A yellow scarf tied over her head screamed happiness. Her long-sleeved T-shirt with the foundation's logo looked a couple sizes too big and covered well-worn jeans.

He didn't know her, but he had a feeling the heavy, lace-up boots were her go-to footwear. A soft humming followed the back and forth motion of her broom as her body twisted. She actually looked more like she was dancing than sweeping.

He wasn't sure he'd ever met someone who enjoyed

cleaning. She looked up and her eyes went wide when she saw him.

Great. He'd been caught staring. What was wrong with him? Her face lit up with a smile. She waved and laughed. Why was she laughing? He frowned.

She should be afraid of him, like everyone else in town—but, no, she was carrying on like they were having a grand time. The lightness of her laughter floated in the air. He could almost see it reaching for him.

"You caught me. I'm a full-on dork. Dancing with the broom." She looked across the space between their cabins. The barn where he had found them was on the other side of his cabin. "Belle wasn't joking when she said we'd be in your backyard. Hope having a baby move in next door won't cramp your bachelor lifestyle." She smiled again.

Silence settled around them. She raised an eyebrow as if she expected him to say something. Making sure she saw his frown, he made eye contact before he had to look away from her. The horses were waiting for him.

He closed his eyes. She was just being polite, like a normal person.

"Damian, I was joking. If you have a problem with us living here, please let me know."

"No. It's fine. I have the horses on a schedule." He forced his attention back to her to prove it was no big deal. Why was it so hard to ignore her like he did everyone else?

"Tío." Cassie came out of the back door, rescuing him. "Mom asked if you could put this in your truck and take it to the burn pit." She held a cardboard box full of items they had cleared out of the cabin. "There are a couple of bags that need to go to town for recycling. Can you help me?"

Taking his opportunity to escape, he took the box and put it in the bed of his truck. Cassie returned with an overstuffed bag. He took it and tossed it in the back of Belle's work truck.

"Where are the others?" Then he could leave.

"There're a couple on the side of the house. Mom says we're just about finished. Are you coming over for dinner?" She followed him around the corner. "We've already started making dishes and pies for Thanksgiving. It smells so good."

"No." He grabbed two of the bags with one hand. Cassie, Belle's oldest daughter, grabbed the other.

"Oh." She paused and her shoulders slumped as if he'd disappointed her.

He sighed. "I would, brat, but I didn't get to work with all the horses today. Next time."

She perked up and ran at him. Dropping the bag, she threw her arms around his waist and squeezed. "Are you coming into town for Thanksgiving tomorrow? Mom said Tío Elijah and Tía Jazz will have Daniel there. He'll be one week old on Thursday."

"Hey. I tend to scare babies." He let his bags hit the ground. All the kids running around in his family now days made him nervous.

Loose hair fell from Cassie's braid. As he pushed it back, his heart did a little uptick. She looked so much like her mom at this age, he couldn't help but want to protect her in ways he hadn't been able to do for Belle. "Thanksgiving at Xavier's and Selena's is a huge event."

"But they are family. He's your brother."

"You know I don't go to town or do big groups."

Narrowing his gaze, he studied Cassie. She had always been mature for her age, but there was an unusual level of concern in her eyes. "What's wrong?"

"Nothing." She squeezed again, then stepped away. "I just wanted to make sure you knew I loved you. We all love you. And I've been worried."

His heart did a weird flip. "About me?" That was the last thing he wanted.

"We've been learning how important it is to let the people in your life know you love them. Especially when they're sad. And I saw that soldiers…" Tears hovered in her big eyes—eyes that matched both his and Belle's.

"Oh, sweetheart." He pulled her into his arm and against his chest. "I'm not sad. I like being alone."

"Well, I wanted you to know that we love you and would like to see you at dinner. Maybe we can have a small dinner, just us, here at your place. I don't want you to—"

He cupped her face, making sure she looked him in the eye. "I'm good. I promise. I'll call if I ever get that sad." He rubbed her head and pulled her into a tight hug. "Okay, Mini-Belle. I'll put dinner with you on my calendar. Sometime after Thanksgiving."

On her tiptoes, she kissed him on the cheek.

"I've got the bags," he told her.

"Okay." Then, with one more hug, she joined the other kids. She was growing up fast and he was so proud of Belle and the mom she'd become. His mother would have loved those kids.

Belle had accomplished so much despite Frank's best efforts to push her down.

He tossed the bags into Belle's truck and made his way to his. He was exhausted and his leg was hurting.

"You have everyone fooled, don't you?" Lexy was at the base of the steps with a smirk on her face.

"Excuse me?" He had no clue what she was talking about.

"I know your secret."

His gut somersaulted a couple of times. There was no way she could know his father's death was his fault. No one knew.

Placing one hand on her hip, she gave him another genuine smile. Not the fake ones people threw at him.

"I don't have any secrets." *Liar.*

"They all think you're a big tough loner, but you're a total softie. Your niece loves you very much."

Relieved, he snorted. "She doesn't know better."

"Children are pretty smart about that kind of thing." Her gaze shifted downward. "Is your leg hurting? Do you need to sit? Come up here. The rocking chair is comfortable. I hope I can get another one. I can see peaceful evenings in the near future, watching the sun go down. It's beautiful out here."

He gritted his teeth. He must have been shifting his weight. He hated that anyone ever saw a weakness in him. "I'm fine."

She moved closer to him. "Is there anything I can—"

"No." Taking a step back, he held his hand up. "I need to go."

Her mouth opened, but he turned his back to her and rushed to his truck.

Out of sight, he rested his forehead against the cold glass. *"Arriba."* He tapped on the bed of the truck and Hansel jumped in, straight up from the ground.

When he opened his door to escape, he saw the small stuffed horse that Jonah carried everywhere. Grabbing it, he slammed his door shut and headed to the back porch. At the corner of the cabin, the screen door opened. *"No te muevas,"* he told Hansel, telling the dog to stay.

Lexy looked up as Belle came through the back door with a plastic bin in her arms. He leaned against the wood siding of the cabin, out of sight. He wasn't strong enough to say no to another invitation to dinner from his family.

"Lexy, look! I found some old Christmas ornaments I tried to put up at Damian's once. Surprise, surprise, he ignored them." She paused. "The cabins would make a perfect picture for a baby's first Christmas."

Lexy laughed. "I love that idea. Living in apartments makes it difficult to go all out."

"We love decorating the ranch. But wait until Selena gets a hold of you. Like she's not busy enough raising triplets and running the city. She turns the whole town into a winter wonderland—which is a pretty amazing feat in south Texas." Belle shifted the bin to her other hip. "You can use these, and I'll get you more if you want. Over the years, we've collected all sorts of decorations for indoors and out. You won't have to buy a thing to make Jessie's first Christmas a spectacular one."

With all the drama, Lexy hadn't even thought about this being the baby's first Christmas celebration. She smiled wistfully. "My mother's favorite thing was Christmas Eve at our church. Our choir put on such a beautiful program. There's something so special about Christmas music. We all sang until mom got too sick."

"It was my aunt's favorite too. I'll stack the bins here

on the back porch, then you can go through them after Thanksgiving. And y'all have to join the church choir."

Belle set the bin against the wall, then jumped up to sit on the railing and settled in for what looked like a long talk. Damian could return the toy later. He turned toward his truck, but the floppy pony stared back at him, rightly accusing him of being a coward. He dropped his head.

Maybe he was. His father had called him that often enough, and worse. He wanted to leave, but he couldn't take his gaze off his new neighbor.

Lexy faced the horizon, the sun highlighting her coppered skin. "I'm not sure I'll be here long enough to bother decorating for the holidays."

"Even if you move on to another job sooner than anticipated, you'd still be here through Christmas," Belle replied, confusion threading her voice.

"I mean in this cabin."

Damian frowned. He rested his shoulder against the rough wood of the cabin. This wasn't any of his business.

Lexy had her back to him. She lifted her hair and adjusted her ponytail. "It might be easier if we moved to town for now. I don't want to intrude on Damian's space longer than necessary. He's made it clear that he doesn't want us this close."

The dying sun caressed the beautiful curve of her neck. He should let her know he was there, but then he would have to tell her that the real problem was that he liked her too much.

No, he'd have to give her other reasons. It wasn't her. Well, it was, but not the way she thought… He didn't even understand himself.

She took him back to his middle school days. Everything about him was awkward and inadequate.

Somehow, in just one day, she'd made him aware that he wasn't as content with his life as he liked to pretend. He knew who he was and his limits. There was no changing his DNA.

From his earliest childhood memories, he'd learned how to survive. The loss of limbs meant it took more time, more practice, more energy to get things done—but that was okay. Being stubborn enough not to quit was the only good lesson he'd learned from his father.

His father. That was a load of guilt he would have to carry alone.

He rubbed his shoulder. Sometimes little actions he took for granted now hurt like all get-out. But he'd never questioned his masculinity. Not until last night, when he'd found himself on his barn floor, looking up at the most beautiful sight he'd ever seen. It had been a new type of dream, but she was real. Too real for his peace of mind.

It shouldn't matter. Her moving in next door wasn't going to change anything.

He knew Belle worried about him, but this little trick wasn't going to domesticate him.

A woman like Lexy would want more from a man, deserved more. Pushing away from the wall with a grunt, he went around to the front and tossed the floppy pony, Bucky, into the porch swing.

Without a backward glance, he made a straight line to his truck. He needed to clear his head. The hinged to his truck door squeaked.

"Damian!"

Belle's voice stopped him hard. How had she heard

that? He didn't turn to her. His gaze stayed on his goal. The barn. It wasn't far. It was on the other side of his cabin.

"Damian." Her breath was short. "Are you leaving?"

He bit back the sarcasm to reply. "I need to get back to work."

The signature clicking noise made it clear she was frustrated with him. With a deep breath, he released the door and pivoted to face her. Great. Lexy had followed her.

Hands fisted at her hips, Belle stared him down. "You're being rude to our new guest."

Lexy stood behind her, shaking her head. "No. It's okay. We've already interfered with his day. I didn't mean to get in the way. Maybe this was a bad idea." She turned to Belle. "You have other cabins, right? Or we can find something in town."

He forced a frown. "You're fine." A smile would be too suspicious. "You're not in my way. I just need to take care of my animals."

"Are you sure? We haven't completely moved in yet. I could find something in town."

"It's better for everyone if you're out here." He pointed at Belle. "She can leave the ranch without worrying. Stay. It's good."

"Okay. Thank you, Damian."

He gave her a quick nod to acknowledge her words, then went back to his goal. To get away from her.

"What about tonight?" Belle wasn't going to let him go easy. "We're going back to the big house to make dinner and to get ready for tomorrow's feast. You should join us."

"Thanks, but no time." He tried to sound pleasant,

but the look on her face told him he hadn't been successful.

"Tomorrow's Thanksgiving, Damian. You'll go into town with us, won't you? The whole family is meeting at Selena and Xavier's house. Now that your brother is home, we should all go."

"They also open their door to the entire town. I'll pass. I told Cassie I'd join y'all for dinner some other night. Invite my big brother and his family to your place some other night and I'll join you." He opened his truck door and climbed in. "You know I don't do big crowds."

She twisted the corner of her mouth but nodded.

This was why being around people was so hard. He was destined to disappoint them.

Lexy followed Belle back into the cabin. The other woman's disappointment was clear. Had her being here made it worse?

"Well, that went much better than expected." Belle washed her hands at the sink. Her gaze stayed on the horizon out the kitchen window. "He really likes you."

Lexy snorted in disbelief. "That's him liking someone?"

With a nod, Belle leaned her hip on the newly scrubbed kitchen counter. "He can't tolerate being around people. You gave him a chance to get rid of you and he didn't take it. Believe me." She pointed a finger at Lexy. "That, my friend, is a big deal."

"He was just being nice."

Belle laughed. Cassie and the herd of small people came into the room. "Tío Damian is only nice to us. He's never nice to other people."

One of the twins climbed onto the one good barstool.

"He frowns and never talks to people other than Belle and us. He likes you."

The youngest girl nodded her head. "Maybe you can be his girlfriend, and he'll be happy. Like Tío Elijah and Tío Xavier."

"Yes!" One of Belle's stepdaughters clapped. "Daddy smiles more now that he loves Belle. Tío Damian needs a girlfriend."

"No plotting." Belle put her hands on her hips. "Not everyone needs a boyfriend or girlfriend."

Cassie, her oldest, leaned on the small island. "But Mom, you're happier. Wouldn't it be nice for Tío Damian to have someone too?"

Shaking her head, Lexy found her words in the chaos of ideas. "Sorry guys. You have the wrong girl all the way around. Your uncle has zero interest in me, and I have other people in my life that I need to focus on right now."

Her sister laughed. "Don't blame me for your lack of a love life. But I agree that Damian doesn't seem to be happy with us being here. He's so not Lexy's type."

"What do you mean, not my type?" Okay, that sounded defensive. "I don't have a type. If I like someone, I like them. Anyway, I've had a hard time managing a second date, so it's more likely I'm not *his* type."

With a shrug, her sister turned to the door. "You date stuffy men you think are safe."

Lexy wanted to argue with her sister, but there was an audience. So, she just gave her the look.

The youngest of the group and the only boy leaned against Belle's leg. "Tío Damian didn't shoot at anyone like people say. He likes animals, and he's nice to us. He can be friendly."

"Enough talk about Tío Damian." Belle picked him up and tickled him. "Will y'all be joining us for Thanksgiving? Xavier, Damian's Brother and his wife Selena will be hosting dinner in town. A few of the foundation employees with be there, including Hunter Martinez. You'll be diving with him. Xavier has a big Victorian home close to the beach and open their doors for everyone."

"Oh, no. We couldn't intrude. We'll plan a quiet dinner out here. It's the perfect place for us to give thanks."

"I understand. We can be a bit much. But, if you change your mind, it's an open invitation." She wrote out a few things on a notepad. "This is the address and our numbers in case you need anything. Need me to bring out any supplies?"

"No." She looked at her watch. "I think we'd enjoy a drive into town. Thank you for everything you've done to make us feel welcome. It means a great deal to us."

Belle hugged her. "Just call if you need anything." She turned to the kids. "Who's ready to go home and make pies? Cabbage, spinach and pickled beets?"

Voices of protest and other suggestions surrounded Lexy as Belle laughed. Jonah slipped to the floor and ran to the door. The girls followed him.

Belle touched her arm as she went to the door. "Lexy. I'm serious about Damian being good with you living here. Please don't feel like you're intruding or unwanted. He's…" She sighed and looked to the ceiling. "He's had a really hard time of it. Life has given him the raw end of every deal since his mother died. It's not an excuse, but don't take it personally. Damian has always been the loner. Then he was the one to find his father dead and that seemed too much for him."

What was Lexy supposed to say to that?

Belle's features softened and she smiled. "This is not any sort of attempt to play matchmaker. I'd be happy if he talked to anyone outside of the family. I don't expect a grand love story. Sorry about the kids. I hope they didn't make you uncomfortable."

"No. They're cute. It's a reminder of how simple life can be. You're sure we're not disturbing him?"

"Oh, you're upsetting his nice little world, but that might be good for him. Sometimes we all need to be pushed out of our comfort zone. But if he really had a problem with you here, he would have told me. Y'all are good."

Good might be a stretch. Until she knew what was going on with her sister's ex, she couldn't rest. The worst part was that Steve was her niece's father. Her own father had died when she was small, and Naomi's father had left before she turned a year old. Neither of them had any memories of their fathers.

She hated that legacy to pass into the next generation. How did she change that? Men couldn't be forced to be good and upstanding. Were there any good ones out there? Her mom had claimed her dad had been, but she had no evidence of that. It was easier to make someone a good guy when he'd died young.

They did exist, though. Quinn was proof of that. Was it in her family's DNA to repel the good guys?

Case in point: she was already drawn to Damian and he was about as emotionally unavailable as a man could get. What was wrong with her?

Chapter Five

The smell of sweet potatoes, cranberries and roasted turkey breast filled the homey cabin. Close by in the living room, Jess sat on a blanket surrounded by brightly colored toys that rattled and beeped. Gretel lay flat on her tummy, her nose resting between her paws, her ears up as she watched every move the baby made. Jess threw a stuffed panda to the edge of her blanket and Gretel pounced and pushed it back with her nose. The baby laughed and threw another toy. They played the game over and over.

Lexy finished the dishes from all their morning prep while Naomi took a much-needed nap. Jess had been fussy for most of last night, just settling in at dawn.

The window over the farm sink framed the cabin next to them. Grazing cattle spotted the pasture beyond. Lexy wiped her hands dry as she scanned the area between Damian's home and the barn. She'd caught glimpses of him working different horses throughout the morning.

Did he really spend all his days alone with no one but the animals to talk to? Today was Thanksgiving and no one should be alone. She understood avoiding big crowds and she shivered at the thought of venturing out in public on Black Friday.

But total isolation couldn't be safe or healthy. Humans had a core need to connect with other people.

She swung Jess up and over her head. "We are going to make sure Mr. I-Don't-Need-Anyone is not alone for Thanksgiving dinner."

Several mason jars filled with candles swayed from the overhang of her porch, filling the November afternoon with the scent of fresh apples and honey. It was almost warm enough to wear shorts and flip-flops, but she just couldn't do it.

Gretel trotted next to her, tail wagging. "You excited to see your boyfriend?" She patted the dog at her heels. The intelligent amber eyes stayed on her and Jess.

Across the yard at the barn, Hansel stood at the door with his master, his tail thumping fast and furious. He looked up at Damian, as if waiting for permission. One slight nod and the dogs leaped at each other, jumping high into the air. Hansel ran to the side of the barn and Gretel gave chase.

Jess laughed at their antics. They came around the other side of the barn, running low and fast. Hansel had something in his mouth as he jumped into the tree, then leaped down.

As soon as he landed on the ground, Gretel rammed her body into Hansel's. They went rolling and tumbling across the yard in an end-over-end tangle of fur.

"Wow. They really go after it." After watching the dogs for a while, she finally turned to Damian. He was staring at her. Her belly did a stupid somersault.

"Uhm… I came over to tell you that dinner will be

served at two o'clock. Just a nice quiet Thanksgiving with the three of us. You'd make four, which is perfect because our table seats four and we don't want an unbalanced table with an empty chair. Empty chairs are very sad."

Damian acted as if she hadn't said a word. Breaking eye contact, he pointed to the dog. "She's doing okay?"

"Naomi has followed your direction line by line. I've never seen a dog like her. It's like she and Jess can talk. She's amazing. I don't know what we'll do without her when we leave."

"They need to have a purpose. They help me with the horses and ride out with me. This breed of dog requires lots of action." The two dogs came running around the barn again, the floppy toy going back and forth in a tug-of-war.

"They have to be the fastest dogs I've ever seen. Did you see how high he jumped into the tree? I looked up the breed. How long have you had them?"

"Hansel was with me in the Middle East. He was military trained for search and rescue. But he lost the sight in his left eye when I lost my arm and leg." He leaned his shoulder against the barn, never taking his eyes off the pair playing in the yard.

"It took some work and Belle was behind most of the fight to get him home. Gretel is deaf. Her training was never completed. She was going to be euthanized, but a guy I know in San Antonio got in contact with me." He shrugged. "I think she misses being around people."

He clicked his fingers twice and both dogs snapped to attention and waited for his command. One small motion with his hand and they both ran to him and sat.

He gave them each a treat from his pocket and tossed them the toy they had been fighting over.

"I thought you said she was deaf."

"She's super intuitive. I made sure to have my hand where she can see it. It's the reason she's always looking at you. That's her way of listening."

Without another word, he turned into the barn. It was as if he'd suddenly remembered he wasn't supposed to talk to her. Well, too bad. She followed.

At the end of the long aisle, King tossed his head and nickered. Along the way, a few other horses had their heads out over their doors. Damian stopped by each one. There was only a handful of horses in the barn. There had to be over twenty stalls.

"You don't have many horses here for the amount of space."

"There are a few others turned out. I try to give them as much freedom as they can handle. I never work with more than six or seven at a time." He stopped at King's stall, but unlike the other horses, King flattened his ears and backed away.

Damian moved back. "Let me hold Jess and see if he comes back to visit with you."

Sure enough, as soon as Damian and the baby were on the other side of the aisle, King returned. He made a low soft rumbling noise and reached his muzzle out to her. Gently she touched the end of his soft nose and ran her fingers down his long face.

"Hey, boy. Why are you so rude to Damian? He's just trying to help you." The stallion rubbed the side of his head against her arm. She couldn't help but laugh. "He's like a giant kitten."

"For you." Relaxing against the wall on the opposite

side of the corridor, he shifted his weight off his prosthesis. "Have you been around horses?"

"Before Mom got sick, we spent hours a week with them. I was on a polo team. My mother grew up with horses in Mexico. They had thoroughbreds and raced them. My mom loved horses."

Her eyes burned as she remembered their last day at the stables. Her mom had tried to be so brave, assuring her they'd be back once she was well again. "When the chemo treatments started making her sick, we had to sell my mare, Luna, and give up the team."

King lowered his forehead and leaned on her. She scratched him behind the ears. "You're a sweet boy, aren't you? Pretending not to like people."

She almost laughed at the similarities between the horse and the man. Being attracted to the wrong kind of males was definitely a pattern in her life. Why couldn't she find a nice man at church who liked her just the way she was? Was it really too much to ask?

King nudged her, then turned and trotted to his turnout. Tail high, he looked at her and snorted, then came back, tilting his head for his ears to be rubbed again.

"Yeah, I see your game," she whispered in his ear. "You get me to let down my guard, then you turn on me. Bam. Blaming me for your hurt pride or whatever it is that keeps you from trusting people. That's your problem, isn't it? You have too much in common with him." And here she was again, trying to get him to join them for dinner. But it wasn't a date. It was Thanksgiving. No one should be alone.

There was no dating in her near future. Not with Steve's drama still hanging over them.

"So, do you want to go out? Are you comfortable with that?" Damian asked her.

Startled, she darted her gaze from King to him. "Uh. No. I don't think it's a good idea for either of us. This is just Thanksgiving dinner."

One dark smooth eyebrow arched high and his full lips twisted to the side as if he found her amusing. "What does taking King to the round pen have to do with Thanksgiving?"

Heat rushed her neck. "Round pen?" Now he thought she was a complete idiot.

"Yeess." He said it slowly, as if he were explaining to a young child. "I asked if you'd be comfortable doing lunge line work with him in the round pen." He nodded to the horse. "One, he doesn't care that it's Thanksgiving, and two, he's a bit big for your cabin. Unless you thought I was talking about something else? Lexy? What did you think I was asking you?" There was a spark in his eyes telling her he had his suspicions and he was probably correct.

"Oh, you mean to take him out of the stall?" She needed to straighten out her thoughts before she got herself in trouble.

"Hey, there you guys are." Naomi walked toward them. Jess reached for her mother. Taking the baby, Naomi smiled. "Are you visiting the pretty horses?" She looked up. "I'm assuming my sister is browbeating you to join us for dinner. We have plenty and an empty chair." She kissed her daughter's forehead. "No homemade pies, but we picked up a fresh apple pie from the cutest bakery in town. I'm sure it's better than anything either one of us can do."

The scowl on Damian's face made it clear that he was not on board with the whole family dinner thing.

"Actually, your timing is perfect." Lexy cut off any denial before it could sprout. "Damian was about to let me take King out to the round pen and give him some exercise."

"Then I'll take Jess back to the cabin and let you two have fun." Naomi winked at Damian, then turned and bounced out of the barn, the dogs at her heels.

His frown dug in deeper. "What did she mean by that?"

"Nothing. Just ignore her. Is this his?" A halter and lead rope hung on a hook between the stalls.

"Yep." He walked closer and held out his hand containing an alfalfa cube. King snorted and tossed his head.

Laying her hand on the horse's neck, Lexy whispered as if sharing a secret. "I know you want that sweet treat. He's much nicer than he looks, I promise."

The horse and man snorted at the same time. She couldn't stop the giggle. Covering her mouth, she clasped her lips together and bit them.

Damian quirked an eyebrow. "You think this is funny?"

Relaxing, she petted King's neck as he gingerly took the cube from Damian's palm. "You have to admit it's cute that y'all share the same cynical outlook."

"Let's see if you're able to work the same charm on him as you do me. I have a feeling that, in a couple of hours, I will be sitting at a table with you and your sister eating turkey and pie despite saying no."

She slipped the halter over King's muzzle, then secured the clasp along his jaw. "I have yet to hear you say that word. So, I'll take it as a yes."

"Watch his ears. They'll warn you if he's about to get upset."

She shot him a look that made it clear she understood Horse Communication 101.

"Sorry. They said he would attack without warning, but I've never seen him do that. He gives me plenty of signs and I make sure not to corner him. I think that's been the problem. He panics if he feels trapped. People tend to get impatient with animals and expect them to just do what they're told. But I have to admit, I've never seen him this calm. Are you sneaking in at night and slipping him sugar cubes?" His voice was still low and deadpan, so it took her a second to understand what he said.

"Was that a joke? And you agreed to eat dinner with other humans. This is a day of giving thanks for unexpected blessings."

"I have not agreed to join you for dinner."

"Baby Jess and Naomi are now expecting you to fill the fourth chair. And think of Hansel and Gretel. Would you deny them this time together?" Moving out of the barn and into the full sun, she felt its warmth on her skin. Damian led the way to a round pen about fifty yards from the barn.

He opened the gate. "Just keep him at a walk for now. Nothing fancy."

With a nod, she rubbed under the stallion's big curved jaw. His coat was sleek and smooth. "He's no fun, is he? No wonder you put your ears back at him. Really? Nothing fancy? You were made for fancy."

Damian pulled himself up on the railing and leaned over to watch them. She winked and moved to the middle of the round pen. Unlatching King's lead rope, she held her arm out to see what commands he knew.

The big horse followed her hand signals and moved to the railing. His walk was open and smooth until he came to Damian. Stopping, he threw his head high and flicked his tail. Damian remained still, not even changing his expression. "She's all yours, big boy."

"Did you just act like you have the power to give me away?" The two males looked at each other, ignoring her. "Seriously. King, if you want to spend time in a battle of wills with Damian, you don't need me for that." She moved to the gate. The horse nickered and moved past Damian. With his tail arched high, he watched Lexy. Smiling, she clicked, and he extended his step.

Each time he passed Damian, he looked at her but flicked his tail. She couldn't help but laugh.

Damian rested his elbows on the top railing and watched Lexy move King through his paces. She held her right arm out and used her body and hands to tell him what she wanted. The horse's bloodlines shone through with each movement of his muscles. This was the reason so many people wanted him, despite his surly unpredictable attitude. But time was running out. If he couldn't be handled, he'd have no value to his owners— and that was not good.

The rascal had been acting out of control and wild. He just hadn't wanted to be bothered with people. The poor animal hadn't understood that his life had depended on his compliance.

But now—since the first morning she'd interacted with King, Damian had seen clear progression. Lexy had the stallion trotting to her command. This would be a much better update to the owners than he had hoped.

Little Ms. Lexy was very dangerous.

Holding both arms out, she walked to the horse and he stopped. She rubbed his forelock and whispered so low that Damian couldn't make out what she was telling the horse. Probably complaining about him.

Other than one side-eye look, King ignored him. The horse was loving the attention from her—but, then again, Damian was finding himself in the same boat.

He needed to focus on the horse and dig deeper into the stallion's history. "I'm starting to think that there was a woman involved with him at one point. If King lost her in the accident, that might explain some of his behavior."

"You really love these animals."

Not having anything to add to the conversation, he just made a noise in agreement. Lexy continued to talk as she went through a short grooming session, and then released King to his stall.

She glanced at her phone. "Okay. I'm going to wash up and help Naomi with the last-minute stuff." Walking up to him, she stopped less than a foot away and looked him straight in the eye, her chin up and her hands on her hips. "We'll see you in two hours."

There was a small twitch in the corner of his lips, but he managed to keep a straight face.

Lexy sighed. "Say 'Yes, ma'am,' and 'Thank you.'"

It became a staring contest. He knew he was going, but he didn't have to let her know how easily he gave in. Stupid pride. That's all it was. "Yes, ma'am."

With a grin, she turned. Her ponytail swung around. Just like King's. "See ya soon."

"And, Lexy."

She stopped and narrowed her eyes at him. "Yes?"

He gave her a slight nod. *"Gracias."*

She stood a little straighter. *"De nada.* Now that wasn't difficult, was it?"

He chuckled but refused to answer. With a wink, she left.

He made his way to the cabin. His leg was killing him. It had been hours since he started this morning and he hadn't taken the time to adjust the stockings.

Sitting down in the one chair he had in the living room, he took off the riding leg and removed the layers of socks. He soaked up the sweat with a towel, then tossed it in the washing machine for his daily load of laundry. Other than a small table in the kitchen, most of the cabin's living space was taken up with workout equipment.

He massaged his leg. Then, standing, he used the crutch he kept in the cabin to go to his bedroom. The only change he had made in the cabin since moving in was to turn half the second bedroom into a huge bathroom to accommodate his new lifestyle with one arm and leg. The luxury of a huge, double-headed shower with benches, bars and no door had been the best gift to himself. The tub that sat in the corner was perfect for long soaks where he could wash out his prosthesis lining while he relaxed in the warm water.

That's where he wished he could be right now, but he knew without a doubt that Lexy would be knocking on his door if he dared not to show up for her dinner.

Why was he able to ignore everyone else in the world, but three days after she showed up in his barn, he was doing whatever she told him?

He was as bad as King.

Stretching out on his bed, he pretended he wasn't going anywhere. But he knew he'd soon be putting on his walking leg and heading over to the cabin next door. Maybe he'd ask her why her car was always hidden out of sight. He sighed.

No, he would not ask, because he didn't care. Life was easier when he wasn't involved in other people's business. She'd be leaving soon and that was a good thing. For all of them.

Chapter Six

"It's such a beautiful day." Standing on the edge of the porch, Naomi took a deep breath and spread her arms wide.

"Eating outside was a great idea. You should have waited, though. I could have helped move everything." Lexy placed the pitcher of tea on the small table that Naomi had moved to the porch. "You've always been so creative." On the center of the table was a small pumpkin overflowing with wild vines and goldenrod flowers that had been growing wild around the cabins.

Her sister shrugged. "You know I can accomplish something without your help."

"Naomi, I never—"

"I know." Hand up, her sister cut off her words with a smile. "Sometimes I just need to prove to myself that I can do stuff on my own. Plus, I like making pretty things."

"Well then, you outdid yourself." Lexy looked to their neighbor's cabin. "Should I go check on him?"

"You can't help yourself, can you?"

"What do you mean? I invited him to dinner, but he

had a really busy day. Maybe it was too much and he needs help."

"You and this drive to take care of everyone. He's a grown man who has lived alone out here for over two years. Go inside and check on Jess. You can wake her up and get her dressed. It would be my guess that he'll be here by then. I imagine he's one of those people who, if you tell him to be there at two o'clock, will be heading this way at one fifty-five. If you go over now to offer your help, he'll be insulted."

Lexy rolled her eyes. "Fine. I'll play the good aunt and get the baby ready."

Going into the room Naomi and Jessie shared, Lexy found Gretel sitting next to the crib looking up at the baby, who was standing with her hands on the railing.

"Oh, look at you!" Over her shoulder she yelled for her sister. "Naomi!" With a huge, two-toothed grin, Jessie bounced, then fell on her bottom.

Naomi rushed into the room. "What is it?"

Jessie reached for the rail and pulled herself up again.

"Oh, she's standing. Look at her!"

Lexy took out her phone and snapped photos of the milestone. "Such a smart girl."

Gretel barked and her tail thumped against the floor. There was a knock on the door.

Naomi went to her daughter. "That's Damian. Go on out and I'll get Jess ready. We'll be there in a minute."

"Lexy. Naomi?" The deep masculine voice carried from the front door.

"You invited him," Naomi said. "Don't leave the poor man waiting. We'll be out in a minute."

Lexy wasn't sure why, but a desire to flee out the back door hit her.

"Lexy?"

Taking a deep breath, she went to greet their guest. "Happy Thanksgiving."

His thick black hair was combed back, the ends touching his collar. The left sleeve of the pullover shirt was rolled up. The jeans looked starched. He wore shiny black boots that zipped up the side.

He stepped back so she could join him on the big porch. "Happy Thanksgiving." He held up a pecan pie. "My mother taught me never to go to dinner without bringing something. This is the one thing I make every year for Thanksgiving. It's my mom's recipe, but no matter how I try, it never seems the same." He looked to the table. "You moved it out here. That's nice."

He seemed nervous. She took the pie he offered. "It looks perfect. Neither of us are much good at baking. Too much exact measurement and order for me." She laughed, but it sounded forced to her ears. "Sit down. I'll take this in. Do you want tea? I can bring you a glass with ice."

"Sounds good, thank you." He went around to the chair by the railing and sat. His body relaxed into the farm chair.

Putting the pie with the one they had bought, Lexy filled three glasses full of ice and joined him on the porch. She sat with her back to the wall. Pouring them each a tall glass of tea, she smiled. "I'm glad you made it. We were inside when you got here because Jess was standing for the first time. She had pulled herself up in her crib. We got a little excited."

"Worth getting excited over. It's a huge milestone. I don't remember the first time I did it as a baby, but I remember the first time I was able to stand on my own after the amputation. It's a great feeling."

The screen door opened. "Hi, Damian."

Jess clapped and grinned at him.

"Hear someone's been accomplishing milestones." He smiled at the baby. Gretel ran to the bottom of the steps and leaped on Hansel.

"Yes, sir. This little girl is growing too fast." Naomi slipped Jessie into the high chair across from Lexy. The baby reached out to Damian. He smiled and took her hand. Her little fingers wrapped around his calloused thumb.

Naomi broke a roll into small pieces and gave a few to Jessie.

"I hope it's okay that I moved the table out here. The porch has more space than the cabin and the weather is begging to be enjoyed."

"I appreciate it. The leg doesn't always work well in small spaces."

Baby Jess offered a piece of bread to him. Making outrageous sounds of pleasure, he pretended to eat it. Happy with his antics, Jess kicked and slammed her tray.

He might have everyone else fooled, but there was more to the story than that he just hated being around people. Now she was looking for a reason to like him. She needed to derail that line of thought. "Are we ready to go ahead and eat?"

Lexy started to stand, but Naomi waved her back. "Today I want to serve you and Damian. I've been doing a great deal of thinking these last two days and you don't understand how grateful I am for you both."

Damian's brows went up in surprise. "Me?"

She nodded. "Without knowing us, you let strangers stay in your barn. You've allowed us to move in next door. I don't think I have ever felt safer or more peaceful than here." She wiped at her eyes. "Anyway, I'm going to serve both of you, so sit back, relax, and I'll bring out the dishes." She turned back into the house.

Damian looked up to the rafters. "The mason jars are new. Never seen them used like that before. Smells nice."

"We found a case of mason jars in the pantry and coiled wire. In town we picked up the candles and a pumpkin. I would have just used the pumpkin as the centerpiece. She found the vines and flowers growing around the cabin and made that." She pointed to the floral arrangement overflowing from the pumpkin. "Naomi is so creative. She could make a living with her ideas."

He nodded, then looked to the sky.

She rubbed her thighs, trying to ease her twitchy muscles. Silence usually didn't bother her. "It's a perfect day for being outside. It's good we're taking advantage of it since rain should be hitting us tonight."

She closed her eyes and suppressed a groan. Great, she was now impressing him with her talk of the weather.

She glanced at the door. "Maybe I should check on Naomi. She might need help."

"I'm sure she does, but she made it clear she didn't want it."

"But it's too much. There's nothing wrong with helping someone."

"Unless they don't want it. The best way to learn what you can handle is by taking on too much and finding a way to make it work. Nothing wrong with falling a few times." He leaned back and rested his arm along the railing.

Jess offered him another piece of her roll. He took it and made funny faces and sounds. They carried on a nonsensical conversation that was more interesting than anything Lexy had offered. Finally, the door opened.

"Happy Thanksgiving!" Naomi carried a large tray she had made from old barn wood. "I think we might have enough to last the rest of the winter." She laughed. "We didn't want to miss any of our favorite memories. What's your must-have dish? I hope we made it."

"Stuffing with cranberries. It was the only time we had that, and my mom made it from all fresh ingredients." He leaned in to take in all the plates and bowls full of food. There was a shadow of a smile, like a long-ago memory that was hiding from view. "That's what I smell. I loved the scent of cranberries with a gallon of sugar and oranges." His brow wrinkled. "I think she crushed pineapple in the mix too."

Setting the tray on a bench, Naomi back inside and brought out a second tray. She moved mismatched plates and bowls to the table. Starting with sliced turkey breast, she added green beans with bacon, sweet potatoes, carrots, creamed corn, mashed potatoes, stuffing and, lastly, the bowl of cranberries with slivers of orange rind on top.

"Yay! That's how Lexy makes it. All fresh. The stuffing is boxed. Not having a full turkey, we just went with a boxed stuffing that was super easy and fast." She bit her lip and sat down. Leaning in, she whispered, "It was made in the microwave fifteen minutes ago." She made a face of horror.

"My favorite kind." He winked at her sister.

Naomi held her hand out to Lexy and took Jessie's little fingers with her other. Damian followed suit and took the tiny hand between his thumb and index finger. Lexy was on his left side. She offered her hand, then thought he might not want to touch her with his arm.

She froze for a moment, her hand hanging in midair, not sure what he expected of her. He looked up and smiled, then placed his elbow in her palm. The skin was warm under his lightweight cotton sleeve.

"Damian, would you lead us in prayer?" Naomi asked.

Lexy saw a flash of panic hit his face. She'd seen him stoic, stubborn, concerned and calm, but it surprised her to see any kind of fear. He didn't want to pray out loud. "Naomi, may I pray over our meal today?"

"Sure." Her sister replied, not having a clue she had scared the man with her simple request.

"Father, we thank You for Your abundant blessings, mercy and grace. We thank You for the food on this table, this land that surrounds us and the deep ocean at our door. Let us always keep in our minds and hearts that all gifts come from You. Father, thank You for each morning that brings a new day of hope. Thank You for the rest and shelter in the night.

"Dear Lord, grant us hearts wide open to see, hear and feel all this beauty You have provided for us because of Your love. Please send love and help to those who are hungry and alone, sick and suffering, or living in war and violence. Open our hearts to Your love so that we might offer it to others. May we be good stewards of all Your creations and of the talents You have bestowed upon us. May we be faithful servants in all You ask of us. Your will be done, we ask this in Your name."

Out of habit she gave a slight squeeze of her hands and whispered, "Amen."

Her sister repeated it and lifted her head. Damian flexed his elbow, his head down as if continuing in his own silent prayer.

With a deep inhale, he let his breath out slowly and raised his head. "Thank you." His voice sounded as if he hadn't used it in a long time.

Naomi picked up the platter of turkey. "Now it's time to load our plates," she announced.

Silence fell for a short time as the dishes were passed around.

Damian pulled out a switchblade-type knife from his pocket and used it as a utensil. Lexy hadn't even thought about the difficulties of eating with one hand.

"Since it's Thanksgiving, we each have to share four things we are thankful for." Even though it was a square table, Naomi acted as if she were at the head.

"Four? Why four?" Lexy scooped cranberries over her stuffing.

"One is too easy. Three is cliché. Plus, it's things we are *thankful four*." She laughed. "See what I did there? I guess we could do seven. Would seven be better?" Naomi rested her jaw on her fist.

"No. Four is good. You start." Lexy took her first bite of the savory turkey. Damian was ignoring them and playing with Jess between bites. Gaze back on her sister, Lexy made a point not to look at him. Just because a man played with babies didn't make him the kind of guy she should be interested in. He had too many issues, and she had too many plans.

He was probably just bored and passing the time.

Her sister set down her fork. "First, I'm forever thankful for my baby girl and our first holiday season together." Her eyes went all soft as she watched Jess play with Damian. "Second," she turned to Lexy, "I'm so, so thankful for a big sister who will drop everything for us to make sure we're safe." She reached over and squeezed Lexy's hand. Then she tilted her head and smiled at Damian. "Next, I'm also deeply grateful for a man who let two strangers and a baby sleep in his barn for the night. Thank you for the shelter that night and for the one we have now. And last, for homemade pecan pie and vanilla coffee. The little things that make life so sweet."

With a flourish of her forkful of sweet yams, she gave a pointed look at Lexy. "Your turn—and you can't repeat anything I've said."

"Seriously?" She added three more carrots to her plate. They had forgotten asparagus. She knew they'd missed something. But that would not help her with her list. There were so many blessings that if she took it too seriously, she'd cry. She would not cry in front of Damian. That would be embarrassing.

"Lexy." Naomi poked her in the shoulder. "Are you trying to tell me you don't have anything to be thankful for?"

"Oh, Naomi. There's so much, I don't know where to start." She took a deep breath. "I'm grateful for a mother who gave me the best baby sister who has gifted me with the best niece ever." She intertwined her fingers and rested her chin on them. "Then there's a grumpy cowboy who's gone beyond being a good Samaritan."

That got Damian's attention. With a slight tilt of his head, he gave her a quizzical look.

"You introduced me to King and reminded me of my love of horses and of all the time my mother and I spent with them. *Muchas gracias, vaquero solo.*"

"De nada," he said softly, then stared at his plate. He loved his life as a loner, so why did it sound so sad when she called him a lone ranger?

"One more, Lexy." Naomi wouldn't let her slide.

"I'm thankful for a boss who gave me a job I love and gives me the opportunity to travel around the world and take my sister with me. There. Now it's Damian's turn."

"Me?"

They both nodded and waited. He looked down. His lips pursed. "Okay." He pointed at each of them with the short knife. "One, two and three." He ended with Jessie. "I'm thankful you're here so I'm not eating my pecan pie by my sorry self. My mother's pecan pie recipe is four."

Then he stabbed a slice of turkey and stuffed it into his mouth.

"I don't think that counts as four. We are kind of one unit. So Lexy, Jess and I are one. Your mother's pie is two." Naomi held up two fingers of her left hand while she took a bite of her roll.

He sat back and made a disgruntled noise. "My dogs and my horses."

"Those are good." Her sister nodded and smiled. "But why?"

"Why?" He wasn't happy about Naomi forcing him to talk.

Lexy didn't want Naomi pushing him. "The dogs are great. We are definitely grateful for Gretel."

"Oh yes. We love that dog of yours. What about the

horses? You don't actually own any of them, do you? Why are you grateful for them?"

Lexy watched him closely. He looked to Jess as if she had the answers, then his gaze went to the sprawling landscape. "No. They're with me temporarily. Their owners are frustrated with them or something has happened to them that means they need extra care. I guide them so that they can work in the world of humans. Once they're healed, they go back." He turned to Naomi. "Without them, I wouldn't have a purpose. These cranberries are some of the best I've ever eaten."

Heat climbed her neck. Why was she blushing at his praise? "Thanks. Have you ever had a horse you couldn't help?"

"There was one I was worried about. Last week I thought he might be my first failure." A slow lift to the corner of his lips could almost be called a smile. "But then God planted a fierce woman right in my barn while I wasn't looking. Now there's hope he can make it."

"King?"

He nodded.

Warmth settled over her skin at the praise. Taking her focus off of Damian, she adjusted the food on her plate. With their plates just about finished, Naomi leaned over to Jess and wiped her hands and face. "So. You save horses. My sister saves marine life. Y'all really have a lot in common."

"What are you doing on the ranch? Other than babysitting me?" Damian asked.

"You are the last person on this planet that needs babysitting," Lexy answered. "But I'm happy to run your errands for you. I travel to locations—or future locations—the foundation is working with. Being part of a group that is having a positive impact on the oceans is mind-boggling.

"My job is twofold. I collect data and feed it to the computer so that the scientists can sort through it and adjust our recommendations. I also document with photos. We use the images in seeking grants, education and outreach. On the side I have a blog that highlights the importance of our underwater world. Plus, I'm a freelance writer."

"She's a professional diver," Naomi interrupted proudly. "She's had articles in *World Travel* and several other publications about diving and the work the foundation does. And I know it's just a matter of time till she lands an international gig. She has queries in with *National Geographic* and some other important nature magazines."

Naomi pointed her fork at Lexy. "You know, she finished college and gained the highest level of scuba certification there is while taking care of our mom and raising me?" Naomi leaned forward and whispered as if Lexy couldn't hear her. "She kind of scares me. But man, she's an amazing person."

"Naomi. Stop." Lexy could see that Damian had no idea what to do with this information.

Jess hit her tray and started fussing. Naomi grinned and stood up. "On that note, I'm taking my daughter inside to change and get some floor time. Maybe we'll work on her mad standing skills. Go ahead and enjoy the rest of your meal. I'll make some coffee in a few minutes and bring out the pies."

Lexy closed her eyes and listened to the tall grasses surrounding the cabins as they rustled in the wind. Suddenly she could hear the ocean waves. She sat up tall. "How close are we to the beach?"

"See that rocky outcrop?" He pointed to a high point on the horizon. "That's our closest point. You can be there in less than five on horseback." He scooped the last bite of stuffing and cranberries into his utensil using the deep edge of the plate. Chewing, he sat back and studied her.

She fought the urge to squirm. Why was he just staring at her? "So. Uhm. You never go into town? Not even to see your family?"

"Nope."

"Why?"

He sighed and finally took his gaze off her. The silence was heavy, and she waited. For what she wasn't sure. He'd made it clear he didn't want to talk. Fine. She could sit and stare off into space with the best of them.

The day was perfect and Monday she'd be diving with Hunter. Diving often saved her when life became too overwhelming. She closed her eyes and gave thanks again for the amazing blessings given to her.

"When I go to town, I get pulled over a lot."

She blinked. "Why?"

"Drunk driving."

She gasped. "I've never seen you drink anything at any time, let alone—"

"I don't drink. Ever."

"Then why are they pulling you over?"

"When I first got back to town, the prosthesis was new, and I stumbled a bit. I lost my balance and fell a couple of times. I didn't move as easily as I do now. With my father's history of raging public intoxication and then Elijah's battle with alcoholism, it was easy for everyone to assume I'd returned from war with PTSD and was drinking it away. I got one of two looks. Suspicion or pity. I'm not sure which is worse."

"It's horrible to be accused of something you're not doing. They still stop you?"

He shrugged. "I haven't been into town for over a year. It's easier if I stay out here. I don't want to be around people, and they don't want to talk to me."

She nodded. "That's one reason I started diving. No one can talk to me. It even clears out my own thoughts." She stood and stretched her back. The dogs had been playing and running the whole time they ate. Now Gretel jumped the steps and put her paw on the door. She glanced back at Lexy, who laughed. "What? Spent enough time with your boyfriend? You need to check on the baby?" She opened the door, and the dog slipped into the cabin. "Poor Hansel looks heartbroken."

"I warned him." Damian stood and rolled his shoulders.

"What? That Gretel would leave him for a cute baby?" The dog lay down with a huff and rested his muzzle on his crossed paws.

"That she'd want more."

Lexy chuckled, but when she glanced up at Damian, his face was grim. Okay, so not a joke.

He stood next to her. Hansel sat straight up and wagged his tail, waiting for Damian to give him something to do. At the man's hand gesture, the dog ran to the porch of the other cabin, then came back with a small canvas backpack. She recognized it as the one Damian always had close.

"What's in there?" Hansel brought it to Damian and waited for him to take it.

"Leg paraphernalia." He went to the bench and sat down, resting the pack next to him.

"Is something wrong?"

"No. He just needs something to do and I usually keep this with me. When I got the pie, I forgot the back-pack. I've never done that before." He looked at her as if it were her fault.

The door opened and Naomi came out with the baby and a blanket. Gretel was close as usual. Handing Jess to Lexy, she spread the green-and-blue blanket in the corner of the porch. "The coffee is brewing. How do you like yours, Damian?"

"Just a touch of sugar and milk."

With a nod, she went back inside. With Jessie play-ing on the floor next to the attentive Gretel, Lexy sat on the handcrafted bench. "Thank you for letting her serve you. I know you're ready to go back to your space."

He grunted and pulled out a hard rubber toy with strips of faded, worn cloth on the sides. He threw it off the porch and Hansel lunged midair and caught it. He and Lexy sat in silence and watched the baby play with Gretel. Poor Hansel was alone in the grass with his chew toy.

Naomi set a tray on the table. A bit stiff this time, Damian stood and went back to the spot he'd claimed earlier.

"Thank you, Naomi." He used his special knife-spoon thing to eat the pies.

"Oh my. This pecan pie is so good! You made this?" Naomi looked shocked.

His face kind of twisted into a smile. "Yes, ma'am. Belle's is better."

Lexy thought of the cookies and pies her mother had

made. Neither she nor Naomi had been able to reproduce them. "There's something about a mother's touch that makes them perfect."

"Thank you, ladies. It's time I got back. I have to feed before I turn in for the night."

With a few goodbyes, he and Hansel walked to his place.

"You should make him dinner. Just the two of you."

"What?" Swinging her gaze from Damian's retreating form to her sister, Lexy gaped at her. "Why on earth would you think that a good idea? I have never met a more emotionally closed-off human being in my life."

Her sister waved her off. "You don't like people either. This way of life is what you consider paradise. You have the ocean, the wide-open land and animals. A small town you can visit and go to church in. This, sister, is your utopia. And he is beyond cute. It's not his injuries, is it? I would think that kind of thing wouldn't bother you."

"No. But, seriously, have we not met the same man? He might as well have a neon sign blinking NOT AVAILABLE."

Her sister smiled. "We'll see."

"No." Lexy shook her head as she went back to watching Damian make his way to the barn. Her sister was so far off the mark on this one. And they weren't staying, anyway. "Promise me, Naomi. No men, no dating, no flirting until we get this mess cleaned up with your ex. Neither of us can afford to be in a relationship right now. As soon as your passports get here, we'll be going to South America and then Australia."

"Whatever." Her sister crossed her arms. "I just think you are missing a perfect opportunity."

Lexy shook her head. Oh, she saw an opportunity all right. One to get her heart broken. Not happening. She had plans, and Damian De La Rosa was not a part of them. No matter how cute he was.

Finally, alone, Damian sat on his back porch. His prosthetic leg next to him, he massaged the area around his knee. Relaxing into his chair, he leaned back and sipped his coffee. This had always been his favorite time of day. Unwinding and watching the sun sink down behind the horizon. Hansel stretched out next to him.

This world he had built was perfect for him. He could hear the horses in the barn. But now there was a new sound. The little family next door had disrupted his world and he feared that, even after they left, he would never be the same.

Chapter Seven

$\sim\!$

With the soft tinkling of a tiny bell, Lexy stepped into a Victorian Christmas novel. The hundred-year-old Port Del Mar Livery and Mercantile was a special world that took her to another time and place.

Christmas was overflowing. Green garland wrapped around the columns, while red ribbons, pinecones, cranberries and sticks of cinnamon gave the store an old-fashioned holiday feel.

The smell of leather tack and fresh baked goods added to the charm of the old wood floors and vintage glass counters. A huge mural along the back wall depicted a scene from the Old West when it was still a working livery stable, in the early days of Port Del Mar. She stepped closer to examine it.

The details of a lamp glowing through a nighttime drizzle drew her into the artwork. The storm swirled around a lone rider coming in for shelter. A woman stood at the door, lamp in hand, braving the weather as she guided the man to safety.

The painting reminded her of Damian's barn. At least it hadn't been raining the night they had come looking for a place to rest. But he had provided a warm place out of their personal little storm.

"Welcome. Can I help you?" A woman in her mid-forties with a bright yellow scarf holding back a halo of dark curls came out from the back room. Her smile was warm and genuine as she stopped behind the glass counter. Lexy noticed hunting knives and fishing gear at one end and a wide assortment of old-fashioned candies and fudge on the other.

"I'm Lexy. I work for the Yamazaki Foundation. Belle sent me in to pick up an order for Damian d—"

"Oh yes. I was expecting you. We were just talking about you moving out there. Welcome to Port Del Mar. You're going to fall in love with this town. We visited over fifteen years ago and never left. We sold our business in Houston and bought the store. It had been boarded up for years, a huge mess." She took a breath and laughed. "Sorry, more than you wanted to know." She held out her hand. "I'm Joyce Keller."

She smiled but didn't pause long before continuing. "Belle said you might be needing some scuba gear too. We carry a whole section in our sporting goods area. You're a scuba diver, right? If there's anything you want, but don't see, we can order it." She stopped and waited for Lexy to reply.

The idea that they had been talking about her was uncomfortable. A downside of small-town living. Everyone was in everyone else's business. Another reason for Damian to stay away. Lexy turned to the window that faced the shoreline across the street.

Streaks of pink, orange and red filled the sky as the sun caressed the sleepy little town in the soft morning light. Lexy had left her sister and Jess sleeping in the cabin that now smelled of cranberries and pumpkins, along with the fresh scent of oranges, instead of old rags and mold.

"Lexy?" The sweet smile fell.

"Sorry. Yes. To all the above."

"I'll have the horse feed and Damian's package loaded in the truck while you look around."

The neatly organized shelves called to her, giving her the urge to touch and explore all the textures, colors and scents. Handmade toys were arranged in neat baskets.

On the other side were colorful handmade sweaters, gloves, socks and scarves. Jeans and boots filled another section, as did saddles and bridles.

Next came camping gear, then fishing. A whole wall dedicated to rods and reels. Everything was covered, from bay fishing to deep sea. This store was amazing. A poster advertising the Saltwater Cowboys caught her attention. That was the fleet of recreational boats that the De La Rosa family owned. Did Damian have anything to do with the family business?

A lightness hummed in her body as all the possibilities of her new adventure settled around her. The store was a beautiful to-do list ready to be put into action.

"Hello?"

The tentative voice stopped her before she reached the scuba gear. Pivoting, she found a lanky teenage boy with short dark hair cut close to his perfectly shaped head. He blinked, then looked down. His right hand went across his chest and rubbed his left arm. His long basketball shorts revealed a black-and-red prosthesis on his right leg.

He shifted his weight, looking to the left, then back at Lexy. Another blink, and he looked to the right.

"Hello. I'm Lexy. Do you need help? The owner went to the back. She should be—"

"That's my mom. I…umm… I was wondering if you really work with Mr. De La Rosa, Damian. I heard you live next door to him and his barns."

"I do."

One corner of the boy's lips twitched. His shoulders rose, then fell. As if gathering his courage, he lifted his chin and looked Lexy in the eye. His ebony skin glowed. "I would… Could I… Is there anything… I can help you. I mean, I could go with you and help unload. I used to do that all the time. Do you need help with something at the ranch?" He crossed his arms then stuffed his hands in his pockets. "I heard you were coming in to pick up the De La Rosa order. I want to meet Damian, but he doesn't ever come into town. I… He does so much, and he's lost his leg, too, and a hand. My parents don't want… I mean, they worry about me, but I want… I'm so sorry. The words in my head and what's coming out of my mouth are not matching. You must think I'm an idiot."

"No." Lexy stepped closer and rested a hand on his shoulder. "It's okay. You seem very nervous. I do live next to Damian. You want to talk to him?" She wanted to tell the boy that Damian would love to talk to him, but that would be a lie. "He's not very talkative."

"I know. But I think if I could just be around him and watch what he does. How he does everything. My parents are so afraid of me getting hurt. They're super-protective since I lost my leg. It was an infection that went crazy. I kept telling everyone I was okay because I was playing baseball and didn't want to miss a game. That was a little over a year ago. So, they feel guilty and keep me from doing anything that might hurt me. They don't believe me anymore when I say I'm okay."

"I'm so sorry. I'm not sure how Damian can help you."

"He rides horses that no one else can handle. He plays the guitar and other instruments. He helps run a ranch and trains dogs. He lives on his own and does whatever he wants. I need to meet him and find out how he does everything." He pressed his lips into a straight thin line and shifted his weight. "To show my parents I can take risks and live my life again."

With a nod, Lexy gave the boy a gentle smile. "He is pretty amazing. I didn't even realize he was missing his lower leg when I first met him. What's your name?"

His shoulders dropped and he looked down. When he came back up, there was a slight grin. "Sorry. I don't know what's wrong with my brain. Hello, I'm Beckett Keller." He offered her his hand.

Lexy took it and laughed. "It's okay. Do you go with customers and help unload? Will your parents let you?"

"I used to." He sighed. "Now they don't even let me work in the store."

"Beckett Lamar Keller! What are you doing? You should be at the house."

"Mom. I heard you talking about Mr. De La Rosa. So I was asking her if I could help…and maybe go out to the ranch with her. I need to get out of the house."

"There is no reason for you to go. How would you be able to help? I'm sorry, sweetheart, but I'm afraid you would be in the way."

Lexy hated seeing the boy shut down. "I would love to have the company."

"We don't want to bother Damian. He doesn't like people on the ranch."

"But I'd stay with her." Perking back up, he pointed to Lexy. "I just want to see how he does all the things he does. Please. I want to get my life back."

Tears hovered on Mrs. Keller's thick lashes. "Oh, sweet boy. Your life is the most important thing to me. I know you want things to be the way they were before, but it's not possible."

"Mrs. Keller. I would love to drive him out to the ranch and show him around the barns. I need to return the pallets, so I'll bring him right back."

"Please, Mom."

Lips tight, the older woman looked from her son to Lexy.

Lexy wanted to reassure the worried mother and support the teenager who felt trapped in his new life. "It will just be a short field trip. I could use the company."

"You'll keep him out of Damian's way? I hear he shoots at people." She shook her head. "No. I don't think this is a good idea."

"My sister and I live right next door to him. I promise any stories about him have been exaggerated."

Joyce's lips twisted, then she sighed. "Small towns tend to do that. Okay. But you'll bring him right back."

"Mom, she's not going to kidnap me. Before I got sick, you wouldn't have batted an eye at me going."

She hugged her son. "Yes. Almost losing you changed everything for me. Promise you'll call me if you have any trouble."

"I promise."

She nodded. "The truck's loaded. Is there anything you need to add before you go?"

"No. When I bring Beckett back, I'll do some shopping. I'll bring my sister and niece. They'll love your store."

Beckett kissed his mom, then grabbed Lexy's hand and rushed out the door as if he were afraid something would stop them if they didn't hurry.

Damian shifted his weight as he stood. Standing at the far end of the attached padlock, the young stallion lowered his head and stared at him. The trust wasn't there yet, but they were closer. The horse's ears flicked to the side.

A ranch truck pulled up outside. Damian frowned at King. "Belle and her crew left yesterday." The sound of the familiar engine pulled at his gut. He frowned at the unwanted feelings. Who else would be in the old truck his father drove?

"Damian?" A sweet voice called from outside. His heart picked up its pace. No, he wasn't reacting to her. He couldn't.

King snorted. "Yeah. I'm not sure I'm buying it either." The stallion raised his head. Straightening his back, Damian scowled at the horse. With a flick of his tail, the stallion trotted into the stall that he'd refused to enter just a short while ago and made a low rumbling noise.

"Traitor. Just like Gretel." He whispered low so that Lexy didn't hear.

"Hey there, pretty boy. This is Beckett." There was a low feminine laugh. "Yes. I missed you too. We're looking for Damian. Have you seen him?"

He loved that she spoke to the horse as if he would answer her. *Wait.* That was not loving. There wasn't anything he loved. Especially about Lexy. She'd brought someone to his barn.

Hidden in the shadows, he leaned against the wall next to the outside tall gate. If he waited long enough, she'd go away like everyone else.

"Damian? Are you there? " Entering his stall, King swung his head over the half door and nudged her as she stepped forward to rub his jaw. "Pretty boy."

Damian moved out of the shadows.

"Oh, you just about scared me, lurking about. I went into town and picked up your feed and a couple of other boxes from Guitar Center." She looked around the horse at him. "Do you actually play?"

He hated that people made a big deal about anything he did, as if he were a two-year-old just figuring out the world.

Without answering her, he went back into the paddock and out the side gate. He made his way to the truck.

Why had she brought someone out to his barn? Belle knew better. Didn't she tell Lexy?

He pulled a feed bag forward, then went under it so he could heft it over his shoulders.

"Damian, we can unload those." Lexy insisted. A tall, lanky boy, with ebony skin and hair cropped to his scalp, followed her.

Damian paused midstep. The teenager wore a prosthesis on his right leg. It had to be the Keller's youngest son. Belle had told him about the boy and asked if he could come out and visit with him.

He wasn't a support group kind of guy and all he'd do was scare a teenage boy. Being anyone's mentor gave him nightmares.

"You have a small tractor. Why don't you use that." Lexy followed him. "We can get this in one load."

"Lexy," he growled, "I prefer physical work. I do this all the time." He adjusted the sack and went to the barn. Dropping the bag, he turned and bumped into Lexy. Her bag slipped from her grip and he leaned over to stop it from hitting the ground.

He closed his eyes and focused on his balance.

"Oh, I'm sorry," she exclaimed. She shifted the weight of the bag back under her control. Then she moved around him and placed it on top of the other. "I didn't mean to sneak up on you."

"You don't have to help. I've got it." The Keller kid was hovering at the door. Not wanting to scare him outright with his glare, he ignored the boy. Maybe that would be enough to chase him away. "Why did you bring him," he muttered. "Sorry, I don't like people at the barns."

"Damian." Lexy glared at him. "He just wants to know how you do everything you do."

They both watched him as if he had some great bit of wisdom. They followed as he made his way back to the truck. Hansel never left his side. Neither did the two interlopers. It was a regular parade.

Deep breath in. He counted to three, then stopped. This wasn't going to get rid of them. They weren't bad visions to be locked away. Going down, he positioned another bag over his shoulder. The boy's dark eyes watched his every movement. He broke and asked, "Do you have a physical therapist?"

"Yes, sir." His eyes lit up like Hansel's when Damian gave him a job to do.

"Do what they say. With training, you can learn to

use other muscles. Experiment. Try things on your own. Different things work for different people." He went back to work.

Behind him, the teenager mirrored his actions and slid a fifty-pound bag onto his shoulder. He wobbled a bit. He held himself still. Then the teen straightened and grinned at him.

"Lexy. He's going to hurt himself."

The teen's smile fell. *Great.* Now he was kicking puppies.

"I'm good." Biting his lip, he took a step toward the barn. "I used to move feed bags around all the time. You know. Before."

His sister's newest resident rushed to the boy's side and helped balance the bag. Lexy looked like a worried mother hen. From behind the teen, she glared at him.

"Your parents just don't want to see you hurt. Let's not do anything to upset your mother." Lexy was soothing the boy.

A disgusted sound came from Beckett. "That's the problem. Everyone is worried I'll hurt myself. Every day I get a long list of all the things I *can't* do."

They made it to the feed room, where he lowered his bag next to Damian's. "Mr. De La Rosa, you don't let anyone stop you, and you have *two* missing limbs."

"Then don't let people stop you. Just don't get hurt on my property. I hate paperwork and doing an incident report would put me in a bad mood. And don't call me Mr. It's Damian."

Making sure to keep his don't-mess-with-me look, he walked between the two. The matching stunned expressions on their faces made it difficult.

Beckett turned to Lexy. "Was that a joke?"

He knew Lexy had not taken her gaze off him. He paused. He couldn't fight his curiosity about her reply. Why did he care? And why was he *not* already in a bad mood?

"Oh, no. He prefers Damian."

He almost laughed. Why did she refuse to take him seriously? Everyone else backed off when he growled in their direction. She laughed at him.

"I meant about being put in a bad mood. This is his happy?"

"He's a total ray of sunshine, am I right?" She laughed. "Come on. He's going to think we're slackers. Let's get this unloaded, then I'll introduce you to my sister and Baby Jess."

Without another word, they finished unloading the truck. When all the bags were stacked, Damian made sure to be heading in the opposite direction. There was no need to drag this out.

"Mr. De La Rosa? I mean, Damian. Can I ask you some questions?"

Dropping his head, he paused, but he refused to turn around and look the kid in the eyes. He was a coward. "No time. The horses are on a schedule."

"Okay. Can I come out next time we have a delivery, then?"

He should tell him no. There was nothing at his place for the kid.

"Please, sir. I'll stay out of your way." His young voice pleaded like his baby sister's had the day they sent her away. It had been for her safety. He needed to send Beckett away too.

"Damian, I'll make sure he stays with me."

He arched his neck and looked at the rafters above

him. "If your parents are okay with it, fine. But," he tossed over his shoulder, "don't expect me to impart any wisdom or advice."

"Yes, sir. Thank you."

He continued walking so that they would know the conversation was over.

"Beckett. Go over to my cabin. I'll be there in a minute."

"Yes, ma'am."

Damian picked up his pace, but not fast enough. Lexy's warm hand touched his shoulder.

"Thank you. I know having people around isn't easy for you, but this could change his life."

"Whatever he expects from me, I'm sure he'll be disappointed."

"He's just looking for inspiration and hope." Her voice was soft and low.

He made the mistake of looking at her. A harsh sound that might have been an attempt by his body to laugh cut through his throat. "Hope? He's come to the wrong place."

"Not true. Beckett sees a strong man living life on his own terms. He needs to know it's possible, and you give him that."

He studied her face. She believed what she said. There was no way to change her mind. He'd learned long ago that people would believe what they wanted and nothing he did could change their perception.

Chapter Eight

More than a week slipped by, and Lexy found that they had fallen into a comfortable routine. She left each morning to cover the agenda for the foundation and was back by late afternoon each day. Whether it was collecting data or taking photos, underwater work was fun, and the hours went by fast.

She was blessed to be able to continue this work while keeping Naomi and Jess safe. Quinn and she had worked out a plan that would have her working at several sites in Argentina for six months, and then Australia for as long as needed.

But today her diving partner, Hunter Martinez, had to leave, so she was home early. Most days she arrived back at the cabin to find Naomi and Jess hanging out at the barn with Damian. Well, not exactly with him, but watching as he worked with the horses. Jess loved the horses and Gretel went to work with Hansel to burn off energy.

That was her hardest time to stay true to her goal of keeping a distance from Damian. It would be so easy to linger and watch as he interacted with the animals, building trust with them. The way he moved, and the low rumbling of his voice made her want to be closer to him.

But once he had the horses adjusted and doing what was expected of them, he sent them away and moved on to the next challenge. There was no long-term commitment in his vocabulary.

In fact, one of the mares had been picked up yesterday, and Damian had given her a note to give the owners when they arrived. He didn't even come out of his cabin. When she asked if the mare's leaving bothered him, he shrugged his shoulders. "There's always more horses."

There was no sign of any of them outside today. Parking the car out of view, she made her way to the cabin. Stepping inside, she frowned. It was too quiet.

Where were they? The last few days, Naomi had been restless. Before they'd come here, she'd been working in a preschool as she took classes. Now she was talking about finishing her early childhood education degree online.

Sunday, at church, Elijah's wife, Jazz De La Rosa told them about an opening at the preschool that would be perfect for her. Maybe that's where she was? But how would she have gotten there?

Lexy looked at her watch. It was nap time for Jess, so Naomi and the baby should be in the cabin. Lexy eased the door closed. "Naomi?" She kept her voice low in case the baby was sleeping. But there was no baby. No Naomi either.

Her heart kicked up a pace. She took a breath and scanned the room for any clue as to where they had gone. Maybe outside?

What if Steve had found them? No. Not yet. He didn't

know about her job on the coast. If he was looking for Lexy, he'd go to Houston. *Where were they?*

Nerves twisted her gut. She forced her breathing to even out. They were here somewhere. They didn't have a car and surely Naomi would have left a note. Her eyes darted around the room, trying to think of any legitimate reason for her sister and niece not to be home.

It was twelve thirty. Naomi wouldn't be expecting her but still, where else would she and the baby be?

Had Jess been fussy, and Naomi had taken her for a walk? Neither of them was used to being cooped up inside so much. What if they were hurt? Her throat burned as she tried to breathe. Her sister took Jess to the city park every day, but this wasn't a park. It was wide-open land with snakes and bulls and all sorts of dangerous things that could—

There was nothing in the house. She rushed through the back door and called her sister's name. *Wait.*

She turned to Damian's cabin. He would know if anyone had come in. He wouldn't allow anyone to take them.

The place where he usually parked his truck was empty. Adrenaline pushed through her veins as she rushed to his door. The only place he ever went was to Belle's, and she was out of the country with Quinn. If he had gone somewhere, Naomi would have been vulnerable.

She went straight to the front door and knocked. Nothing. Two more hard knocks and still no answer. Stepping back, she glanced around. Maybe Damian had taken them somewhere.

No. He never drove to town. But there had to be

a reasonable explanation. She was just overreacting. *Please, God, let me be overreacting.*

Had they gone to the big house or somewhere else on the ranch? She was early, so they wouldn't have worried about her showing up while they were gone.

Moving to the right-hand window, she cupped her hands and peered inside. The room was neat and tidy but there was more workout equipment than furniture.

On the counter in the small kitchen sat a diaper bag. Pink and frilly, it looked out of place in the sparse masculine house. Her breathing eased. They had to be with Damian.

They were safe. She tapped the window. No one was inside. Straightening, she turned to the barn. Where could they have gone, and why was the bag in his cabin?

Now she was just irritated. They could have left a note. Why would he drive them somewhere without the bag? Had there been an emergency?

The barn door was slightly open. Damian's voice reached her before she saw him. "Your *tía* should be here soon. I heard her car. Why do you think she's back so early?"

There was some sweet babbling in response. He was talking to Baby Jess. "Yeah, we need to do something about that rinky-dink piece of plastic she calls a car."

More gurgling and giggling from her niece. Hansel stuck his nose through the door, then sat down and wagged his tail, looking at her inquisitively. She peeked inside.

"Lexy." His voice was louder now, but it still carried the gravelly undertones that made her skin too tight for her bones.

Why did the sound of her name from him do this to her? She closed her eyes and calmed her racing pulse.

"Why are you hovering outside my barn? You don't usually have a problem inviting yourself or others without my permission."

Hansel turned around and went back inside. Lexy stayed still. Being alone with Damian was not good for her. As long as she kept busy and focused, he stayed out of her mind.

"Your niece was just telling me she needs a diaper change." When she didn't respond, he spoke to the baby. "What is that aunt of yours doing, Jessie girl?"

Teeth clenched, Lexy stepped out of the bright light of the Texas sun into the cool shadows of the barn. Blinking, she paused to let her eyes adjust. She wasn't sure where he was. "Why do you have my niece?"

Jess squealed and kicked her legs in excitement. The colorful toys scattered across the exercise saucer clattered as she reached for Lexy. Gretel was lying on the floor next to her. Her tail thumped the ground.

Damian leaned over a half door, a currycomb in hand. He smiled—a real smile that changed his whole face. Were her eyes still not working?

He had dimples and creases that highlighted his eyes. The kind of lines that came from being outdoors. For a moment she forgot how to breathe.

She needed to do something other than look at him. With a quick move, Lexy picked up Jess. Chubby little fingers grasped her ear and the baby gave her a wet, openmouthed kiss on the cheek.

"Naomi got a call from the preschool," Damian explained. "They wanted her to come in for an interview."

Relieved, she kissed her niece on the forehead. "Your

mommy had to be excited." It took an effort, but she made sure not to look at Damian as she talked. "At church, your sister-in-law mentioned they might have an opening and introduced Naomi to the director."

The stall door opened, and she watched as his boots came close. She evened her breathing, then turned away from him to look at the horse in the stall.

The beautiful gray mare arched her neck over the door, trying to nudge Damian. "She was thinking of walking to town with Jessie," he said.

Forehead wrinkled, she stared at him in confusion. "The horse?"

He grinned. "No. Your sister. She had Jessie in a stroller ready to go. I offered my truck and babysitting services."

"You watch babies? Uhm… The rumor is that you shoot at people. You don't let anyone come to your cabin."

He rolled his eyes. "One misunderstanding and I can't live it down. Can't trust most people and most aren't worth knowing. Anyway, folks tend to stay away if they think I'm actually capable of shooting someone for walking up to my property." He rubbed the mare's nose. "Besides, I let you, your sister and Peanut move in next door."

"But babysitting?"

He shrugged and put the brush in a caddy. "I've been known to watch my nieces and nephews. Hey, I was serious about the diaper change, but now that you're here, I'll let you take over. Naomi should be back soon."

With him out of reach, the mare turned to Lexy for attention. Jess cooed and kicked her feet in excitement. Damian stopped at the door. His body went deadly still.

It brought to mind a big cat about to give chase. "Damian?" She whispered, but she wasn't sure why.

He remained silent for a long minute. "I've noticed you always park your car behind the cabin. Out of sight of the road. Is there a reason?" When he spoke, he kept his hard gaze on the road.

"I…uhm." Why was he asking now?

"Are you hiding from someone?" Deadly. His voice had gone low and hard.

Bouncing Jess, Lexy felt her pulse jump. What was happening? "Yes. Naomi's ex, Jess's father. He's into some illegal stuff and it has threatened them. I don't trust him. That's why I brought them with me."

With a quick nod, he acknowledged her response. "Could he know you're here?"

"He knows I work for the foundation, but I don't think he knows about the ranch." Finally, she heard what he'd been seeing. The quiet growl of a motor as a vehicle drew near.

"Okay. Stay here until I come back and I'll see who it is. I'm not expecting anyone, and it doesn't sound like any of my family." He stepped through the door and out of sight.

Lexy held Jess closer and rocked her. The baby was fine, but she had to keep her that way. That meant fighting the urge to charge out to face whatever Damian was worried about. Her instinct was to tell him to back off. This was her problem. They were her family and she would take care of them.

But that was the attitude that had gotten her sister deep into trouble, and it was how their mother had left them with no help or connections.

She closed her eyes and kissed her niece's soft hair.

It would not destroy her to accept help for her family. Leaning against the wall she made sure to stay out of sight. If she had been alone maybe she could have done something, but Jessie's safety came before her pride.

The baby pulled at her ear. In the distance, she heard a car door slam. Male voices rumbled, too far away for her to make out the words.

Was that Steve? She hadn't been around him enough to know his voice. Her gut burned. What would they do if he had found them?

She reached for her phone in her back pocket. She needed to call the police. She stopped and, tilting her head, studied the rafters above. And just what would she tell them? The father of her niece was stalking them? They couldn't do anything about that.

A horse called from the opposite end of the barn. King had his head over the door. He was in his stall because he knew she was in the barn. Needing a distraction to keep herself from confronting Steve, she moved to the horse.

The stallion tossed his head and gave a low rumble. "Hey, pretty boy." Palm up, she offered her hand, careful to keep Jess on the opposite side from the horse.

"Thanks for getting me away from the door. I hate not being the one that saves my little sister." King's ears flicked back and forth, listening to her and to the baby's babbling.

Jess patted her cheek. "Ma. Maaa. Ma."

"Yes, your mother is always getting into scrapes, isn't she?" She kissed the top of Jess's head, then adjusted the baby on her hip. "What we need is for your mom and you to get your passports so that we can head to South America for Quinn. I've always wanted to travel and now I get to do it with my two most favorite people in the world."

The voices outside stopped. A car door slammed, and the sound reverberated through the barn. King lifted his head high, his ears forward. Finally, a car pulled away from the barn.

Please don't let it be Steve.

She had accidentally found this place. It was easy to get lost on backcountry roads. No reason to stress over the unknown. The self-pep talk wasn't working.

She stopped at the front of the barn and waited for what seemed like forever. Finally, Damian slipped inside and the breath she didn't realize she was holding eased from her, but she couldn't fully relax.

His lips were in a grim line. "It wasn't him. It was Red's owner." With his chin, he indicated the stall on her right. It looked empty at first, but a roan was huddled in the back corner. "He thought he had the right to come out to my barn without calling. She's not ready for visitors."

Lexy sagged in relief. Steve hadn't found them.

Damian laid his big hand on Jess's soft curls. The baby smiled up at him, but Damian's eyes stayed on Lexy.

She hugged Jess closer, her mind racing with what could have happened. She didn't have solid plans in place. What if that had been Steve? She needed to prepare, to keep a supply of diapers and food for Jess ready to go in a moment. She needed to keep the gas full and cash on hand… But where would they go? This was the safest place she knew. She didn't know anyone else she could trust with the safety of her family.

Words tickled her ears. Damian had been talking. "What did you say?"

"Nothing." He dropped his hand. The hard line of his jaw flexed.

He was mad at her? Her gaze darted to the barn exits. Which was the fastest escape?

Damian stepped in front of her. "Lexy." His gray-green eyes searched her face, an intensity she hadn't seen before holding her in place.

She forced herself to relax at least a little. They were safe, for now. Her hand went to his arm. She didn't understand the need to connect with him, but it was a strong instinct. She knew without a doubt if it had been Steve, Damian would have helped her.

"Thank you."

"For what? Are you going to tell me what's going on? The more I know, the better prepared we are."

She nodded. Jess kicked her legs and pushed against Lexy. "*Phew.* This little one does need a diaper change." Lifting her head, she met his sharp gaze. "Come inside with me? I'll tell you the whole sorry tale."

With a curt nod, he turned and opened the barn door for her. He stayed close behind, the dogs next to her. There might be a storm on the edge of their lives, but she had never felt more protected. Why did this connection she had with Damian feel so strong?

It had always been dangerous to rely on others, but Damian had her believing it could be different with him.

No, the lessons she'd learned watching her mother count on people who'd then abandoned them were burned into her brain. She just needed to remember them. Getting comfortable was the last thing she could do if Steve and his trouble was about to tear their lives apart.

But how much should she tell Damian?

She glanced over her shoulder and almost stumbled. Damian was close enough to reach out and steady her. Just as quickly he stepped back, putting space between them.

He didn't say a word, but he didn't look away from her either. Could she trust him?

The battle raged. *Yes, trust him with everything. No! No one will take care of your family the way you can. Don't tell him your secrets. Don't open up to him. You'll just get hurt.*

Wordless, they stared a bit longer. Then Jess fussed. Oh, right. She was here to take care of the baby. That was her job.

She would do whatever it took to keep them safe. And right now, Damian De La Rosa was one of her best options.

That was all. There was no great connection that would change her future. Turning, she held Jess closer and went up the steps to his cabin. He opened the door. A small hesitation and she crossed the threshold into his home.

Damian took a deep breath. She was in his home, his space. He scanned the open room. It was clean but sparse. Nowhere comfortable to sit but one chair. He gritted his teeth and went past her to the kitchen. "I'll give Xavier and Elijah a heads-up to keep an eye out for any trouble. Do Quinn and Belle know?"

"Thank you. Yes." Placing a little blanket on the floor, she laid baby Jess down to change her.

He needed something to do. "Coffee?"

"Sure." Her hair slipped over her shoulder as she leaned over the baby and clapped her hands. The sight gave him an unfamiliar ache in his chest.

Uncomfortable, he forced his attention onto the coffee maker. But he couldn't completely ignore the homey family interaction taking place in his cabin. Lexy took a colorful toy from the bag and shook it over Jess until the baby grabbed it. It went straight to her little mouth. The dogs sat on either side of her.

Lexy stood and went to his sink to wash her hands. Her arm brushed his. "Sorry." She stepped away.

He rubbed his hand on the front of his jeans. "Milk? Sugar?"

"I drink it black. You aren't drinking?"

"No." He leaned on the counter. "What do I need to know about the ex? Jess's father?"

She glanced at the happy baby playing on the floor. Her shoulders rose and fell in a measured movement. "Naomi met him in the first week of college. She was so in love. If I stated any concerns, she'd get defensive and say I was still trying to control her life. She pulled away from me. He had her convinced I was too controlling. Over Christmas break, they had an argument and she broke it off. As soon as she was back in school, he was there at her door, convincing her to take him back.

"I didn't know it at the time, but he moved into the house I'd bought for her. Then she calls me. Pregnant. He wanted to marry her, but when she hesitated, he grew violent."

Damian went stiff and his eyes narrowed. "He hit her?"

"Not then. But he slashed her clothes and broke her dishes and her framed family pictures."

"Did she go to the police?"

"No." Lexy pressed her forehead into her palms. "She was embarrassed and blamed herself. I had made it hard for her to be open with me."

"Sounds like you blame yourself too." He took off his hat. Setting it on the counter, he ran his hand through his hair. "You know that manipulative men count on the people they abuse to blame themselves. It's how they work."

"You sound like you have personal experience."

He shrugged dismissively. "We can keep all the ranch gates locked and only people with the code can get in or out. Did he physically attack her? Is that why you went on the run?"

She nodded, holding the warm coffee close in both hands. "He was losing control. She kicked him out but didn't tell me."

Moving to the floor, she sat next to the baby. "When she called crying and upset, I thought that was why she needed me. But it seems he's gotten involved with a criminal element. He's in over his head and apparently decided that the best course of action was to hide from them."

She looked up at Damian. "Two very rough-looking men came to the house. They threatened Naomi and told her to give them the stuff or they'd make it worse for her. They wanted to know where Steve was hiding. She had no clue about any of it. A little later Steve shows up and she said he was worse than before. He accused her of trying to destroy him as he tore up the house."

"4 for 4" MINI-SURVEY

We are prepared to **REWARD** you
with 4 FREE Books and Free Gifts for
completing our MINI SURVEY!

Romance

Suspense

You'll get up to...
4 FREE BOOKS &
FREE GIFTS

FREE
Value Over
$20!

just for participating in our Mini Survey!

Get Up To 4 Free Books!

Dear Reader,

IT'S A FACT: if you answer 4 quick questions, we'll send you 4 FREE REWARDS from each series you try!

Try **Love Inspired® Romance Larger-Print** books and fall in love with inspirational romances that take you on an uplifting journey of faith, forgiveness and hope.

Try **Love Inspired® Suspense Larger-Print** books where courage and optimism unite in stories of faith and love in the face of danger.

Or **TRY BOTH!**

I'm not kidding you. As a leading publisher of women's fiction, we value your opinions... and your time. That's why we are prepared to reward you handsomely for completing our mini-survey. In fact, we have 4 Free Rewards for you, including 2 free books and 2 free gifts from each series you try!

Thank you for participating in our survey,

Pam Powers

To get your 4 FREE REWARDS:
Complete the survey below and return the insert today to receive up to 4 FREE BOOKS and FREE GIFTS guaranteed!

"4 for 4" MINI-SURVEY

1   Is reading one of your favorite hobbies?
     ☐ YES   ☐ NO

2   Do you prefer to read instead of watch TV?
     ☐ YES   ☐ NO

3   Do you read newspapers and magazines?
     ☐ YES   ☐ NO

4   Do you enjoy trying new book series with FREE BOOKS?
     ☐ YES   ☐ NO

Please send me my Free Rewards, consisting of **2 Free Books from each series I select** and **Free Mystery Gifts**. I understand that I am under no obligation to buy anything, as explained on the back of this card.

☐ **Love Inspired® Romance Larger-Print** (122/322 IDL GQ5X)
☐ **Love Inspired® Suspense Larger-Print** (107/307 IDL GQ5X)
☐ **Try Both** (122/322 & 107/307 IDL GQ6A)

FIRST NAME   LAST NAME

ADDRESS

APT.#   CITY

STATE/PROV.   ZIP/POSTAL CODE

EMAIL ☐   Please check this box if you would like to receive newsletters and promotional emails from Harlequin Enterprises ULC and its affiliates. You can unsubscribe anytime.

HARLEQUIN READER SERVICE—**Here's how it works:**

Accepting your 2 free books and 2 free gifts (gifts valued at approximately $10.00 retail) places you under no obligation to buy anything. You may keep the books and gifts and return the shipping statement marked "cancel." If you do not cancel, approximately one month later we'll send you 6 more books from each series you have chosen, and bill you at our low, subscribers-only discount price. Love Inspired® Romance Larger-Print books and Love Inspired® Suspense Larger-Print books consist of 6 books each month and cost just $5.99 each in the U.S. or $6.24 each in Canada. That is a savings of at least 17% off the cover price. It's quite a bargain! Shipping and handling is just 50¢ per book in the U.S. and $1.25 per book in Canada*. You may return any shipment at our expense and cancel at any time — or you may continue to receive monthly shipments at our low, subscribers-only discount price plus shipping and handling. *Terms and prices subject to change without notice. Prices do not include sales taxes which will be charged (if applicable) based on your state or country of residence. Canadian residents will be charged applicable taxes. Offer not valid in Quebec. Books received may not be as shown. All orders subject to approval. Credit or debit balances in a customer's account(s) may be offset by any other outstanding balance owed by or to the customer. Please allow 3 to 4 weeks for delivery. Offer available while quantities last.

▲ If offer card is missing write to: Harlequin Reader Service, P.O. Box 1341, Buffalo, NY 14240-8531 or visit www.ReaderService.com ▲

BUSINESS REPLY MAIL
FIRST-CLASS MAIL   PERMIT NO. 717   BUFFALO, NY

POSTAGE WILL BE PAID BY ADDRESSEE

HARLEQUIN READER SERVICE
PO BOX 1341
BUFFALO NY 14240-8571

NO POSTAGE
NECESSARY
IF MAILED
IN THE
UNITED STATES

He tilted his head back. "Tell me she called the police."

"Not until after she called me. I told her to do that and I would be there as soon as I could. She filed a report, but she didn't have names. I picked her up and we headed here."

She rubbed her temples with her fingertips. "She was so excited about the possibility of this new job. What if he does find us?"

"Where would you go? For now, this is the safest place for you. I can drive her in to work. No reason for her to become a prisoner on the ranch. Xavier can drive her home. You only have one car, anyway."

"You would do that? I thought you never went into town."

"I'll just drop her off, make sure she's safe and come back to the barn. We'll leave early enough to give the cops time to pull me over. Or she could drive. No problem." He narrowed his eyes at her, then looked at the clock. She was home three hours sooner than normal.

"What?" She took the rubber band out of her hair and undid the braid. "Why are you looking at me like that? Did I do something wrong?"

"In all the commotion I forgot to ask. Why are you home so early today?" He needed to move. The well-organized world he had constructed was tumbling down. Going to the front window, he pulled the curtain back. There couldn't be a good reason for her to leave work hours before schedule.

"Hunter, my diving partner, had a family emergency and had to leave. It's a strict policy that we never dive alone, so I came home."

"Could Steve be behind the emergency?"

"No. I don't see how."

She covered her face with her hands and Damian worried she would start crying. Then, leaning over the baby, she threw them wide. "Boo."

How could a father ever hurt the people he loved?

Jess giggled. There was no way not to smile at the sweet sound. How could this guy walk away from that?

"I don't want to become paranoid and see everything as an attack from Steve." Sitting up, she rebraided her hair.

His attention was off the baby and back on her. Her fingers wove her hair faster than he could track. "Just because you're paranoid doesn't mean they aren't out to get you."

Her fingers stopped and she tilted her head to look at him. "What?"

With a shrug he went back to the view outside. "It was a poster in my sixth-grade English teacher's room. He loved posters and I was bored and trapped inside. I would memorize the sayings and look up the words I didn't know." Stuffing his hand in his pocket, he faced her again. She looked so small on the floor with the baby. Easy to break. "Don't worry about hurting his feelings or overreacting. If something feels off, follow your gut. Don't take anything at face value."

His phone vibrated on the kitchen counter. A few strides and he had it in hand. "It's Naomi."

She stood.

"Naomi, I have you on speaker. Lexy is here."

"What is she doing home early?"

"Hunter had to leave," she explained. "Are you okay?"

"Yes! I'm fantastic." Her voice was pitched higher

than normal. "Damian, thank you so much for watching Jess. I start my job training tomorrow and I get to bring her with me. This job is perfect for me. I'll be the teacher for the three-year-old class."

"That's great, sis. Are you on your way home?"

"I have so much to do and plan. I need to go by the store."

"For now, come home. We're waiting for you."

They said goodbye and Damian slipped the phone into his pocket. Had she even realized she had called the ranch "home"? That they had become a "we"?

Chapter Nine

They had dropped her sister and niece at the preschool in the middle of town. Now Damian was driving her to the research location. Fingers, long and tan, rested on top of the steering wheel as he eased the old truck over the rough terrain.

She turned from watching him to force her attention on the landscape outside the window. The horizon stretched beyond forever. Waves reached out to the land, holding on as long as they could before slipping away again. The rhythm settled her heart and gave her a deep peace as nothing else could.

God, let me rely on You. I know You are always there for me, even when I turn my back. Thank You for holding me. She pressed her hand to the cold glass.

"Lexy, it's going to be okay. They already have safety precautions set up at the school. No one gets in without the front desk releasing the lock on the door."

"I know. I was talking to God. Not being in control is hard for me."

He chuckled. "That's why I like staying alone in

my corner. I have a solid illusion of control. Works well for me."

"Then we crash at your barn and move in next door. Sorry. Now you're driving us to work. We've completely disrupted your life. I really don't need a personal escort." She laughed. "Of course, the highlight is, not a single cop pulled you over."

He shook his head and what almost looked like a grin teased at his lips.

"Belle would say it's good for me. Maybe I was getting a little too set in my ways. Plus, Hunter is still out. I'll go out on the boat with you."

Her eyes went wide as she pushed her back against her door. "What? I don't need a self-appointed babysitter."

The corners of his lips quirked up. "That sounds familiar. Jess didn't mind. She has rated me as an excellent watcher of babies."

Oh, no. It was much easier to deny any attraction when he was grumpy and kept his humor under wraps. She turned her focus to the cloudy sky over her right shoulder. "She's a baby. Hence BABY-sitter. I don't need you to hang out all day. I'm not diving."

"Do you need to dive?"

She sighed. What had happened to the silent brooding man? "Yes, but Quinn knows Hunter is gone so he isn't expecting me to do the underwater work."

"I can dive with you."

"You dive?"

"You mean can I dive because of missing body parts?" His smile slipped and his fingers tightened around the steering wheel. "I grew up on the coast. I've dived my whole life."

"Sorry. I didn't mean to—"

With a shake of his head, he dismissed her apology. "It wasn't easy to relearn. After the initial surgeries, I was in Florida for the first stages of rehab. They have a great diving program. It was helpful for overall core strength and readjusting to how I moved on land too."

"Is that the reason you're so good with the horses?"

He nodded. "The only issue I have is getting back on the boat, but it just takes help." His gaze stayed on the road ahead. The ranch pier came into view. The long narrow boardwalk stretched out into the Gulf.

"Thank you, but I don't need help."

"That's the hardest part, isn't it?"

"What?" She studied the details of his face.

"Asking for help."

She closed her eyes and sighed in defeat. "It is."

How did he understand her in ways she didn't even know herself? Uncomfortable, she shifted and pressed her shoulder against the door.

A determined look settled in his strong jaw. "I've been wanting to dive, but I've kept putting it off. Growing up, it was something I did all the time."

"You have gear?"

"Yep. Plus, a new fin I haven't used yet."

"A fin?"

"A specialty leg for swimming. I should be using it. My tanks are checked and ready. So, even if you don't dive, I will. I don't have to follow company policy."

She glanced in the back seat of his truck where she had put her gear to see if she'd missed something.

"Locked box in the bed of my truck," he said, answering her unasked question. "My newest leg is made for diving. The first time I dived I didn't have one. Air got trapped inside the prosthetic and I floated to the surface like a buoy. It was so embarrassing." He made a rough sound that might have been a chuckle. "The guys laughed the whole time they had to work to get the air out."

Biting the inside of her cheek, she held back a laugh. He had probably been humiliated.

"It's okay to laugh. I'm sure those guys are still laughing whenever they tell the story. I had as much grace as a turtle on its back."

"The new leg is airtight?"

"Yep. And it goes from land to water." His left leg flexed. "Never had one that's done that before. They're relatively new to the market. And not cheap. It might be worth more than my truck. It wouldn't do to not use it."

She wanted to ask how he could afford such an expensive piece of equipment, but that would be rude. "That's cool. You're already wearing it?"

"Yep. The little things we take for granted." He winked at her before turning his attention back to the road.

They made the rest of the trip in silence. What must it take to relearn how to move through life all over again?

The private dock came into view. Captain Carlos waved from the blue-striped center console boat, his ever-present smile beaming their way. Living on the coast seemed to make people happy.

Wordlessly, she and Damian gathered their gear. He set his gear on the boat. She gathered her underwater camera equipment from the back seat of his truck.

"That is some fancy-looking equipment."

Unable to keep her excitement down, she grinned.

"I've upgraded the rig. Today is the first day I get to play with my new toys."

"So, we both have new toys. That's always fun. Ready?"

Slinging her backpack over her shoulder, she nodded.

He picked up a duffel from the floorboard. "It's been a while since I've been on the water."

"It's my favorite place in the world. I don't know where I'd be if I hadn't found diving in college. When Mom was moved to hospice, it was my therapy and the best place to talk to God. It still amazes me that I get to do this for a living."

"That's what my horses do for me." He offered a hand to help her board. Chest tight over what they had in common, she searched his face, but his lips were set, his expression closed off again. Did he regret telling her personal details about his life?

Once on the boat, she turned to help him. He handed her his duffel, then leaped from the wooden pier to the boat. Not a single sign that he wore a prosthesis. The dogs joined them.

Gretel hadn't wanted to leave Jess and Naomi, but she couldn't stay at the preschool.

"Good to see you, Damian," Captain Carlos greeted him. "It's been a few years since we've been out on the water together." The men shook hands.

Damian's gaze swept the boat. "This is new." Then he gave a low whistle. "The business must be doing well."

Carlos grinned and caressed the boat. "It is. But this beauty was purchased by Quinn's foundation. With this sweet ride, The Saltwater Cowboys have added scuba diving tours along with the charters and pirate ships."

Just like on land, each of Damian's movements on the boat was precise. He was slower but moved with clear intention. Settling onto the comfy bench, Lexy pulled out her camera. The underwater world let her forget the problems above. "Are you part of the family charter business? You look the part of a saltwater cowboy right now." She took a couple of photos. He still wore his cowboy hat.

Carlos looked over his shoulder. "This one is a silent partner." He laughed out loud. "Very silent. I thought today had been cancelled, so thanks for calling me. With all the Christmas by the Sea getting into high gear, your sisters-in-law will have me dressed up as Santa or an elf if I stand still for too long. How do you avoid all that hoopla each year?"

One brow raised, Damian lowered his chin and stared at him for a long silent moment. Carlos cleared his throat. "Uhm, yeah. So, I need to practice my silent death stare. That's my problem, I talk too much." He turned to Lexy. "So, where to today?"

She handed him the coordinates. "We'll start along the shore of the ranch, then we'll head out about thirty miles to the dive site."

Settling in, she glanced at Damian. "There's an artificial reef we started with the help of Texas and Louisiana. It's a baby. Then another thirty miles farther, there's an established reef that I want to document. We're comparing the growth or lack of. In the 1970s and '80s big companies did a lot of heavy dumping in the guise of creating reefs, but it created a disaster. It did more harm than good."

Damian had his head back. With his eyes closed, the open waters and sky surrounding him, it looked as if the sea was calling to him. The dogs were right by his side. It was picture-perfect.

Carlos opened the throttle as they headed into open waters. Lexy's heart raced at the sight of the endless horizon. This is what she lived for and sharing it with Damian excited her more than it should.

"I thought Quinn's foundation was all about sea turtles," he said, without looking at her.

"That's just a small part. We're global. Clean beaches and healthy habitats are so important to our world. The oceans connect us all and what happens there supports the quality of life we have on land."

"You love what you do."

"Yes." She couldn't take her eyes off him.

Eyes still closed, he turned his face to the sun. She wanted to trace the edge of his profile.

He sighed. "When our passions coincide with our way of life, it's a wonderful thing. To love what you do for a living is a blessing I take for granted sometimes."

"Passion and love. Do you think it's possible to have those in your work and in your personal relationships, or do you have to choose?"

"The ocean makes you a philosopher?"

She smiled. "You didn't answer my question."

For a long moment he stared out to the water. Then he shrugged. "For me, work is the only option. It's possible for others. Belle has found that perfect combo."

"What about Elijah and Xavier with their wives? They seem to have found it too."

"I'm surrounded by happy couples," he grumbled. "I'm not sure about the boys. They had some major obstacles to overcome. They're working on it, but they could still mess it up. It's not for me. I told you. We have to know our limits. I'm too much like my father. My horses keep me balanced. It's best if I stop there."

The idea that he wasn't even open to love made her sad. Why did she want to argue and change his mind? Taking in a deep breath of the salty air, she leaned her head back.

Maybe it wasn't possible to have it all. He was right. They were tremendously blessed to have work that they loved and a passion for doing it every day.

She'd have to be content with that.

As they descended in the water, Damian searched for Lexy. His light barely penetrated the murky layer they swam through. The crackling and snapping sounds of the unseen creatures surrounded him.

A couple more feet and they should be below the fog… And there she was.

A lightness in his gut spread as he watched her propel herself downward. Joy and peace radiated from her and his whole body responded. His heart too.

He had told her that he could live without personal love, and he would, but apparently his heart hadn't gotten the memo.

The water cleared and a world of color and strange life forms came to view. She looked over her shoulder and gave him a thumbs-up. Lifting her large camera, she pointed at him.

He shook his head as she swam under the bars of the old rig, now covered in marine life. He followed her through the huge eight-legged structure. Communicating with simple hand signals, they explored the fantastical environment.

Fish swam up to her, then darted away. Her work

made the world a better place while she put her personal life on hold to make sure her family was safe. She didn't seem to have any problems putting her trust in God.

Light from above filtered through the water, blues and greens surrounded by the bright colors of the man-made reef. A man-made structure God used to provide shelter and protection for His smallest, most delicate creatures.

Earlier, Lexy had said that this was her favorite place to talk to God. It was also the perfect place to listen. *God is our place of safety.* He thought that was in Psalms. His mother had taught him to tell all his problems to God and to trust Him. He had stopped trusting in anything a long time ago. Maybe because he had stopped listening to Him.

Staying close, he helped her take and store samples. He checked his gauge. With a hand gesture, he indicated it was time to make their way to the surface. The sense of space and time was so different under the water.

She went up, but as he followed, something stopped him. Face tight, he looked down but didn't see anything. He tried to go forward again. His heart rate jumped. He was trapped, but he couldn't see or feel anything. Kicking out didn't help. Five…four…three. The most important thing he could do was stay calm.

A hand touched his arm. Lexy had come back for him. He pointed and gestured for her to go up, but she shook her head.

She swam around him looking for the problem. Then she pulled a knife from her pouch and started cutting in the area of his prosthesis. His air was disappearing at a faster rate than normal. Pausing, she offered him her extra mouthpiece. It had the look of an octopus tentacle. She rolled her eyes when he refused.

She went back to work on his leg again, and he twisted to see what was happening. He still couldn't feel anything. Finally, she lifted her hand and showed him a long, tangled fishing line. She had cut it from his leg. With a nod, they both headed slowly to the light above.

Breaking through the surface, Damian dropped his mouthpiece and took a deep breath. Lexy was right next to him. "Thank you. I didn't even see or feel that line."

She nodded. "No one can see them, that's why they're so dangerous. They're why I always have a knife with me. And another reason we swim in pairs." She made her way toward the boat. "Hunter had to cut me out of the stuff on a trip to Mexico."

Once they arrived at the boat, Carlos reached down and helped her up the ladder. Then they both helped Damian climb on board. He heaved his body onto the boat, then removed his tank and flopped on the deck.

"I was getting a bit worried." Carlos squinted in the sun. "Everything okay?"

"I managed to get trapped, and Lexy had to rescue me." Damian closed his eyes. He had gone to protect her. He had become the hindrance. Yeah, he needed to listen to God and stay away from people. "We'd already stayed down longer then we should have."

Slipping her tank off, Lexy took a closer look at his leg. "It was a great dive, until a fishing line snagged Damian. Unfortunately, it's a common problem. I hate that stuff and you can't see it coming." Concern flooded her eyes and she gazed up at him. "It cut through your wetsuit."

"I couldn't feel it."

She sat next to him and gave him a smile that made her eyes shine. "Good thing it was on the fin. If it had cut through your skin, we might have had to deal with sharks. They tend to be docile, but blood changes that."

He almost smiled back. "Carlos, she was pretty fast with that knife. I don't think we should mess with her."

"You had plans to mess with me?" She tilted her head and narrowed her eyes.

"Not me." He chuckled. "My mom raised me to be smarter than that."

Carlos was staring at him, his mouth agape.

Lexy sat straighter. "Carlos? Are you okay?"

He shook his head. "Uhm. Yeah. I just…" He cut his gaze to Damian. "It's nothing, just…"

Damian narrowed his eyes to warn Carlos to stop the path his thoughts were taking. He knew what the Captain was thinking. *When did Damian start laughing and flirting?*

Carlos cleared his throat. "Yeah, well I'll…uhm… just take us back. Anything we need to do before we go home?"

Lexy's brows furrowed, but she shook her head. "We're good, Carlos. Thank you." She swung around to face Damian. "Why are you glaring at him like that? What did he do?"

"Nothing." Ignoring her, he checked his gear.

"Men are so strange."

He glanced up and lifted one brow.

"What? You are. We're chatting and having a good time then you start giving him *el jojo* and he gets all flabbergasted and can't leave fast enough."

"I did not give him the eye." He wanted to glare at her, but that would just prove her point.

"You definitely gave him a look"

There wasn't anything to say to that, so he kept quiet.

"I get the message. We aren't going to talk about it."

She stuffed something in a duffel. "I wanted to say thank you for everything you've done to help us. Not just today, but ever since we got here. Let me fix you dinner. I make a good *chuletas de cerdo a la criolla*. Do you like pork chops?"

"You don't have to cook for me. I have tons to do when we get back, anyway."

"Sure." Disappointment loaded that one short word. She stayed focused on her camera for the trip to shore. He sat back and enjoyed the sun and salt air. Tried to, anyway.

He had hurt her feelings, and it bothered him far more than it should have.

Chapter Ten

Jess squealed, waving a Christmas stocking then stuffing it in her mouth. Lexy laughed. "No, sweet girl. We don't eat the stocking. It's for the Christmas Eve goodies Santa will bring."

Naomi held up two tree toppers. She lifted the glittery silver star high. "Which one? The North Star." She raised her other hand. "Or this one?" It was a dark-haired angel in blue velvet, trimmed with gold.

"We'll put the star on top. The angel will look nice in the window."

Lexy took a picture of her favorite girls topping off Jess's first tree.

"Watch this, baby girl." She plugged in the lights. Their little cabin lit up as bright as Baby Jess's eyes. The baby jumped in surprise, then stared in wonder, the Christmas lights reflected in her wide eyes.

Naomi picked up her daughter and together they went over the details of the small tree. There was a smaller one on the table, along with other unused decorations scattered throughout the living space.

"Let's go outside to see the whole effect." Naomi sounded as excited as a little kid.

It had been years since they had decorated for Christmas. November seventh, three years ago, her mother had taken her last breath. The holidays had gone by in a blur since then, but now they had Jess. Standing outside, shoulder to shoulder with her sister and niece, she stared at their little cabin.

Guitar music drifted from Damian's back porch. Did he really want to be alone? Every time she thought they were getting closer, he pushed her away again.

Reinforcing protective walls could become a habit. She studied his cabin, standing alone and dark in the middle of a huge ranch, separated from the world. No one should be that alone.

Naomi wiped the edge of her hand under her eyes. "She loved Christmas so much. Why haven't we decorated?"

That brought her attention back to her little family. Lexy didn't have to ask who "she" was.

"Grief?" She bounced her hip and kissed the soft curls of the baby who had given them purpose. "Last year we were trying to figure out your new future."

"Another of my mess-ups you had to save me from."

"No." One arm holding the baby, she wrapped the other around her sister and pulled her close. "Maybe poor judgment. But if we let Him, God works it all out for good. Can you imagine our lives without this bundle of joy? I can't. We're a family and we're here for each other. No matter what. We can still have our dreams while supporting each other."

"I saw your last travel blog. The pictures of Belize were amazing. Please don't let me hold you back any longer. You have such an amazing talent and love for what you do. Have you heard back from *National Geographic* or *Nature Conservancy Magazine* yet?"

Lexy snorted. "Believe me, if I had, you would hear my yells of excitement or cries of rejection."

"You'll get in. You're such an inspiration. Travel blog, freelance writer and you dive for a company that is saving the world. A real-life superhero. I want to do something important with my life. I've investigated degrees online. No holding back for me any longer."

"You're a mom. That's the most important job anyone can have."

She smiled. "I love being her mother, but I need to be able to take care of us." A new song floated their way. Naomi took Jess. "That sounds live, but that can't be him. Can it?"

Lexy's gaze went to the dark cabin next to their now-sparkling home. Damian deserved lights and joy too. "I think we should take the extra Christmas decorations to our neighbor."

Naomi nodded. "Great idea. Let me change her, then I'll join you. If I bring her, he won't say no. Have you noticed he's a complete softie around kids?"

She paused at the door. "Is it strange that I can see us living here for a long time? Jess growing up here on the ranch. It would be nice, wouldn't it?"

"Naomi. We can't stay. As soon as your passports come in, we're heading south."

"Because of me." Her sister looked as if she was going to cry again.

"No. Steve caused the problems, but this is a great opportunity to keep you both safe and get a new start.

You know I love to travel. Now I get to travel with you. Quinn and the foundation have been a true blessing."

Her gaze swept the land around them. "Maybe, in a few years, we can come back to the ranch. With Quinn here, I'm sure it will become the headquarters. For now, let's take advantage of the opportunity to travel and see where this adventure takes us."

Giving her sister a reassuring smile, she grabbed a box and gathered all the extra lights and decorations. "Go take care of her but join me as soon as you can. Damian will not be happy with me spreading Christmas cheer into his world."

Before she could even get to his walkway, Damian was on his front porch. Chin lowered. He gave her a look that she was sure was meant to scare her off.

"Merry Christmas!" She stopped at the bottom step. "Belle brought extra stuff from the big house to let us decorate. There was enough for two cabins. So here we are. Jess and Naomi will be here in a minute."

He didn't budge.

"This is the baby's first Christmas and she's loving all the lights. She tried to eat the ornaments and stockings." She pulled out a green ceramic tree with multicolored lights. "I thought this would fit in your window perfectly without disturbing your space."

He stepped closer. "Where'd you get that?"

The white cord dangled to the ground. "It was in the boxes Belle brought."

He took it from her carefully and set it on the table next to his rocking chair. Looking around, he frowned, then disappeared inside.

"Damian?" That was a strange response to the tree.

He came back with a surge protector. Plugging it into

an outlet, he held it up and indicated for her to connect the electrical cord. Without a word she did.

The tree lit up.

Approaching it as if any sudden move would scare it off, he reached out and touched the tips of the lights.

Something was happening and she wasn't sure what it was, so she remained silent and still. After a few minutes, he lifted over his head and looked at the bottom, then smiled.

It was a sad smile. The kind that made her want to hold him close and tell him it was going to be okay, even if they both knew it was a lie.

"This little tree was my mother's. I bought it for her when I was in first grade. There was a school store and the teacher gave us tokens when we did something good. I had saved all of mine and I spent them all on this. I was so proud. My teacher helped me wrap it. Mom gushed over it like I had given her priceless china."

The lights reflected in his eyes, reminding her of Jess earlier. She caught a glimpse of the boy he used to be. Before life made him hard and cynical.

"I thought my dad trashed it. She fought hard to give us a Christmas each year. After she died, he got worse. Dad went on holiday rampages, so we just found ways to hide until he passed out." He snorted and touched the tip of the star on top of the little tree. "Our Christmas wish was for our dad to get so drunk he couldn't scream or—" His nostrils flared.

There was no way she could keep her distance. Three short steps and she was next to him, one hand on his back, the other on his arm. "Belle said she found these in the back of the attic. She wanted to make sure that we could share all the fun of Christmas with Jess."

He nodded. "Sounds like Belle. She tried to hang lights and put a tree up here last year, but I chased her off. Hated Christmas. But I forgot how much my mother loved it."

"Don't let your father steal that from you."

His jaw flexed.

Maybe she had said too much. "I'm sorry. I don't really know—"

"No." He shook his head and squeezed her hand. "You're right. I've let him steal what should have been hers." Just inches separated them.

His eyes were a dark gray-green tonight and they stared at her with an intensity that took her breath. Heart pounding, she waited. For what she wasn't sure.

The space between then closed. The scent of outdoors and ocean that was Damian surrounded her.

His hand slid up her arm and his breath touched her ear. "Thank you."

His voice was low and rough. Every nerve tightened. Like the slow crawl up a roller-coaster.

Click…click…click. Knowing the fall was going to happen but not sure when…

His lips touched hers, so softly she had to press forward to make full contact. His hand went to the back of her neck, not to dominate but to cherish. Was he on the same ride with her? Or was she alone in this connection that surpassed every experience she'd ever had before him?

Their breaths fell into the same rhythm.

Then, just as fast, he separated them and looked to

the barn. As if they hadn't just tilted the whole world upside down. Her lungs were working overtime.

He just stood there all stoic and… And *vaquero solo*.

Had she imagined the thing that had just happened between them? No. They had kissed. Not just kissed; they had connected. And now he… He just stood there like nothing had happened.

Okay. He wanted to play it that way. So could she. She forced a grin. "You're good with the lights and giant candy canes on your porch?"

No answer. His stare into the night was so intense he looked every bit the soldier on duty.

He took a couple steps to the front of the porch as if she hadn't said a word. Was he just going to walk away and leave her babbling to herself? "It's just a few lights and she would love to see your cabin—"

She moved closer to him, not sure if she would follow him out to the barn if he ran. She couldn't do this, couldn't pretend it didn't happen.

"Damian? We just—"

"Don't." One sharp word cut her off.

"I don't understand." It was happening just like she predicted. Her heart was going to break because she let him too close. He had warned her. But she'd ignored the rattle of the diamondback. He wouldn't strike her. Until he did.

"Damian. I'm not going to force myself on you. You're the one that—"

Christmas music interrupted the one-sided conversation. Naomi waved as she came across the yard with Jess. She was filling the cool air with "It's Beginning to Look a Lot Like Christmas."

He sighed and leaned against the railing, as if admitting defeat. "I think I'm about to be filled with the Christmas spirit, with or without my approval." He leaned in and whispered, "Don't you dare tell Belle I agreed to this. As far as she's concerned, I fought till the end."

"Don't worry. I'm the best secret keeper. As far as she'll ever know, I held you down while Naomi wrapped your cabin in tinsel." She tried to lighten the mood, but there was something that couldn't be unheard, unseen or unfelt. They had kissed, and he wanted to act like it didn't happen. Message received.

These few minutes on his porch had forever altered her view of him. Not that she could act on it. Her plan was to be gone by the first of the year. He deserved to be completely loved and cherished by someone, but it couldn't be her. There could be no future for them.

But maybe she could give him back the happy memories he had lost along the way. And if he could remember how it felt to be happy and loved, he could find it again.

With someone else.

As the sisters joined forces and sang Christmas songs, they emptied the boxes full of Christmas joy all over his porch and windows. They had created a cozy nest for Jess next to his chair. Seemed he was on baby duty again. Leaning low he whispered, "I'll be right back."

He slipped into the cabin and grabbed his new guitar. Coming back out, he settled on the rocking chair and tapped his boot at Jess. Her face lit up and she giggled. She was such a happy baby.

Hammering the strings with his index finger, he

strummed with his ring finger. Both women, still decorating the front of his porch, turned to him.

Naomi gasped. "That was you playing earlier? So cool." She clapped. Actually clapped.

There it was again. Treating him like a toddler taking his first steps.

Lexy rolled her eyes and grinned. "Maybe one day he'll be a big boy and go into town all on his own and talk to people." She winked at him.

He grinned as he played a few chords. She was such a brat.

This was his first time to play in front of anyone since the accident. Learning to use one hand had taken a great deal of trial and error—along with bloody fingers.

Christmas hymns were basic and easy. As he played the old church songs from his childhood, the sisters sang in harmony. His fingers stumbled at the memory of his father bashing his old hand-me-down guitar against the bedroom wall one Christmas Eve.

"Damian? Are you okay?" Lexy was close.

"Yep." He had allowed his father's anger to overshadow his mother's love. He started over with "Mary, Did You Know?" One of his mother's favorites.

"Oh. I love this song." Naomi and Lexy's voices joined his, soft and low. Jess went still and listened.

The music soothed the baby while the sisters finished off the explosion of greenery, red ribbons and lights draped over his little cabin. They covered every available spot with the giant wooden candy canes.

The baby's eyes fluttered shut as he strummed. Hansel and Gretel sat on each side of the steps and the barn's low lights added warmth in the near distance. Chin high, Lexy stood, her hands on her hips, looking proud of what they had done to the cabins. This moment was too perfect to ignore.

This fireball of a woman stood in the middle of the world he had created—and she belonged. She made it better. Made him want to be better.

If he had been any other man, a part of any other family, he'd drop the guitar and ask her to stay.

But the youngest son of Frank De La Rosa had no right to her future. He'd been broken way before he left for the service. Broken in a way that couldn't be fixed or rehabbed. His fingers gripped the neck of the classical guitar. Unable to make any more music, he let the silence of nature settle around them.

This moment was a gift. A sliver in time to glimpse what could have been if he were a different man. A man who could be trusted with a family. When they left, he would still have this memory. It was enough. It had to be.

She came to the front of the porch and took pictures. Sitting down on the top step, she petted Hansel. "It's so pretty. I'm sending them to Belle."

He dropped his head. "I guess there's no point in asking you not to."

"It's already done." Her grin had too much joy in it.

He groaned. "I'm never going to hear the end of this."

Naomi tried to stifle a giggle, but he heard it. He gave her a half-hearted glare. He had a reputation to uphold.

"It's bedtime for this baby elf. Good night."

He was alone with Lexy. She was headstrong, bossy and stubbornly independent. All the traits that screamed "Danger ahead." She was too fiery and too…

He was a liar. And not even a very good one. She

was leaving and taking with her a part of him that he'd just found. That was the truth.

"You should come to church with us tomorrow." She stood as if to leave. His heart rate quickened. The urge to keep her close warred with his desire to be alone.

"Any word on the passports?" He needed to remember she had a life out in the world, away from his sad little cabin. She would be leaving. That was a good thing—it was.

"No. It's like being stuck on the railroad tracks. You don't see or hear anything, but you know one's coming. We need to move. The passports can't get here soon enough."

His blood froze at the idea of them leaving. "When are you leaving?"

"As soon as we can." She crossed her arms over her bent knees. "I have to keep them safe. And for now, the farther away we are from him, the better."

Night sounds flitted around them. People thought the country was quiet, but if you paid attention there was more going on than anyone would guess.

"You have to do whatever it takes to keep your family safe."

"Damian, will you promise me something?"

"Depends."

She gave a half-hearted laugh. "You're supposed to say, 'Whatever you ask of me, I will vow it as my honor.'" The British accent made him smile. It wasn't even good, but she didn't seem to care.

He grinned. "I think I'll stick with 'Depends.'" He exaggerated his Texas accent.

She gave a sigh, and her eyes went soft. *Oh, no.* He

was in trouble. He gritted his teeth and waited for the hit to his heart.

"Will you invite Beckett out here? He's gained so much confidence just being around you. He wants to ride. Encourage him, please. Don't cut him off. I think it's good for you, too, to have him around."

He should have known she'd be asking a promise for someone else's benefit. He was pretty sure he'd do anything she asked, but she didn't need to know that. He shrugged. "I don't have a problem with the kid coming out here. But I'm not going to taxi him around."

She laughed.

He scowled. "What?"

"You. Pretending to be all lone wolf, hard-hearted and not caring." She tilted her head and looked up into the night sky. The million tiny white lights draped over his house highlighted her profile. He wanted to devour her beauty.

It wasn't just her features, but the love that radiated from her. Not only for her family, but for the world.

He longed to be even a small part of her world…but he was used to wanting things he couldn't have. She'd be gone soon. He just needed to hold out.

Forcing his attention away from her, he pulled his gaze to the picturesque cabin next door. Not that long ago it had been dark and empty. Now it belonged on the cover of some welcoming home and family magazine.

Yes. He wanted his life to go back to what it had been before she had hidden in his barn.

He shook his head. *Liar, liar.*

She would leave, but he'd never be the same.

Chapter Eleven

L exy cradled the cup of warm tea between her hands. It was hard to believe they'd been here over two weeks. It felt as if this had been their life for years.

Wearing her robe and favorite fuzzy socks, she leaned against the railing as sun greeted the sky. She lifted her sister and niece up in prayer, and then turned her thoughts to Damian. *God, wrap Your love so tightly around Damian that it penetrates his hard shell.*

That man needed to know he was loved more than anyone she had ever met. *Please, God. Open my heart and eyes to Your plans and let me follow Your will.*

This morning her devotion had been Proverbs 3:5 and 6. She liked to think she trusted the Lord with her whole heart, but she knew that, when it came down to it, she held back. She wanted control. Submitting did not come easy. At this rate her path would never be straight.

She needed to work on that. Every cell in her body relaxed as she looked over this grand countryside. Not far away the ocean caressed the shores and an under-water land of wonderment awaited her. And just yards from her doorstep was the barn full of horses that she had come to love.

Yesterday, Damian had taken her riding over the ranch. Just like when they were underwater, they'd moved comfortably side by side without a word, just moving through God's creations.

Closing her eyes, she took a deep breath. There were people she was starting to care about. Why couldn't this be her life? Tears burned as all the worries about her sister flooded back.

How were they going to break this cycle of inviting the wrong men into their family, only to be abandoned or hurt? She wanted better for her sister and for Baby Jess. She prayed that the little girl would never know the pain of loving the wrong man.

Damian emerged from the barn on the back of a beautiful Arabian mare. Once in the round pen, he had her looping and reversing circles. A gentle hand patted her neck as he talked to her. The mare's ears flicked back and forth, listening to him.

She could watch him for hours. This solitary life he lived had its benefits. She was even starting to like it.

With the last sip of tea, she smiled over the cup's rim. If his past actions stayed true to form, he'd be coming over in a couple of hours to escort her into town, even though she'd told him she could handle the Saturday errands on her own.

Their morning trips were a highlight of her day. He didn't talk much, but when he did it was insightful or entertaining.

He had a dry sense of humor that she appreciated. Belle told her he'd always been more reserved than the other De La Rosas, but after their father had died, he'd become a full-blown hermit.

Was it wrong to want to know what had caused him to believe he needed to hide himself away from the world? It wasn't her business, but what she saw was a man instinctively driven to protect. He couldn't help himself. This self-imposed isolation couldn't be good for him.

Rolling her head to the side, she stretched her neck. It was always easier to fix someone else's problems.

King pranced out of his stall into the large paddock connected to it. He stood on the edge with his head high and called out to her.

At least there was one male in her life happy to see her. "Okay. I'll come over. Let me get dressed."

She laughed. Not only was she loving the open spaces and quietness, now she was comfortable talking to animals. Damian was a bad influence.

Inside the cabin, she went up to the loft and slipped on a pair of comfortable jeans and boots. Naomi was talking to Jess in the bedroom off the little kitchen. That baby was a morning person already.

"Hey, sis. I'm going over to the barn. In a couple of hours, we'll go to town."

"You know I'm more than capable of staying out here by myself."

"Humor me. I'd feel better if we were together."

Naomi rolled her eyes. "Oh, please, save me from overprotective people. Go. Go to the barn. Tell Damian hi for me."

"I'm going to see King."

"Right. Keep telling yourself that."

With a kiss on Jessie's sweet cheek, Lexy headed

out the door. Her love for the stallion had nothing to do with Damian.

Pacing along the fencing, King stopped and nickered to her. She laughed as she rubbed his forelock. "Yes. I like you, too, you big lug. What are your plans for the day? Are you going to behave yourself?"

"He's been handling a saddle and bridle well."

Damian's voice caused her to jump. Hand on her chest, she calmed her breathing. "You scared me."

He grinned. "Sorry."

"I'm just on edge." King nudged her with his soft muzzle. "You've worked wonders with him in a very short time." She scratched the horse under his big jaw. "I wouldn't recognize him as the same animal I met our first day here."

He leaned on the fence. "He's been taking the saddle well. Today I thought we'd try a rider on his back."

"Oh, you're going to ride him?"

King leaned into her and closed his eyes in bliss.

"No. I thought you could."

"Me?" Her eyes went wide. "Why me?"

Damian motioned with his chin. "He likes you. He and I were at a standoff until you got here. We'll take it slow to see how he does, but I think you'll be the one who can get past his fears. If you're willing."

"What do you think, King? Are you ready for a passenger, big boy?"

The horse lifted his chin as if to agree, then nudged her. She laughed. "I think that's a yes."

"I'll saddle Rio. He has a calming effect on all the horses, including King." He put a hand on the horse's shoulder and leaned in closer. "You're ready for this." He patted him, then went into the barn.

Her stomach fluttered in excitement. From the moment she'd seen this horse, she had wanted to ride him, but she would never have dared to ask. The idea that Damian trusted her with his biggest project was a little hard to believe.

With smooth efficiency, Damian had Rio cross-tied and ready to go. Halter in hand, he entered King's stall. "Come on in and stay close."

Going through the paddock, she approached King from the opposite side of Damian. "Hey, boy. I'm super excited about this. What about you?"

He handed her the halter. "The saddle is over here."

The stallion stood patiently, only nosing her once or twice as she got everything in place and cinched up.

"Ready?" Damian asked.

Butterflies tumbled as she positioned herself to mount. "Yes, but are you sure he's ready?"

With a nod, Damian stood at King's head and placed his hand under his jaw. She gathered the reins. "We're going to do this as partners, King. Do you trust me?"

She looked at Damian. "Are you sure he won't freak out once I mount him?"

"Look at his ears. His stance. What do you see?"

King bent his neck to look at her, as if to ask what was taking so long. "He looks relaxed and alert."

With one hand on the horn and the other on the cantle, she lifted her foot into the stirrup. A slow deep breath, then she jumped and pulled herself up into the saddle. Not as graceful as Damian, but she was sitting on King's back. He flicked his ears back and forth, listening for her command. Stroking his withers, she leaned over his neck. "We are going to take this slow and easy."

Damian smiled up at her. "I told you he was ready."

"Don't get overly confident. We haven't gone anywhere yet."

He went to Rio and brought the big gelding alongside King. Damian stood on the opposite side of the horse in order to use his right leg for mounting. With one smooth motion, he was atop the big blue roan. Once settled in the saddle, he bent forward to adjust his prosthesis, then sat up and looked at her.

"Shall we?"

"Yes, we shall." And with that, she nudged King and they followed Damian and Rio out of the barn area.

She would follow Damian anywhere if he let her. Not a good strategy for keeping her path straight or her heart whole.

Heading east, Damian thought about taking them along to the water's edge. Lexy loved being in, on or by the ocean. One of his favorite spots was not far away. On the cliff overlooking the water, they could see an endless horizon. The early morning light would be perfect.

He kept a close eye on King. He didn't fully trust the animal yet. If anything happened to Lexy on his watch, he'd never forgive himself.

He had a sense of peace with Lexy he didn't know was possible. He had gotten so accustomed to the fear and anger he carried that he hadn't even recognized it until it began to loosen its hold on him.

"I can't believe you grew up knowing this was yours. It's an amazing legacy."

"I have a hard time believing this is mine at times.

It feels more like Belle and Xavier's. I'm not sure what I would have done if they'd sold it."

She gasped. "They were going to sell the whole thing?"

"My father ran it into the ground. He destroyed the herds my grandfather had built. He misused the land. He had no idea how to handle money. His pride and anger warred for dominance in his life." He scanned the land and sky. "No, that's not true. Finding the next drink drove everything else. The De La Rosa legacy is not something to be proud of."

Pride and anger. Two faults he carried.

"Damian?"

He refused to look over at her. The pity he'd see in her eyes would stab him.

"Damian. I don't see how that can be completely true. I mean about the De La Rosa name. Elijah and Xavier seem like wonderful husbands and fathers. I haven't spent much time with them, but it looks very authentic to me. And Belle. She's great—and she's the one who's been running the ranch for a while, right?"

"Yes. Because we all abandoned her one way or another." He studied the horizon. This was why he preferred to avoid people or sit around with nothing to do. Thinking caused him to face facts he'd rather ignore.

She frowned. "But you all seem so close. I don't see it." Her free hand casually stroked King's mane at the base of his neck. The horse looked relaxed but attentive.

"Y'all are moving well together. You have a natural seat."

"Don't change the subject. Quinn is not the kind of man to marry into a family of degenerates. If no one has told you, then let me be the first."

She paused. Sitting up straighter, she waited until they had full eye contact. "You, Damian De La Rosa, are a good man."

Instinctively he shook his head in denial. "I'm too much my father's son. Of all of them, I'm the most like him. He said it. Xavier and Elijah have said it. Even my mother said it."

He remembered standing in the kitchen, angry over some slight at school and his mother shaking her head as she rolled out the tortillas for dinner. "*Mijo*, let the anger go. You're so much like your father." All these years later, those words from his sweet mother still haunted him.

He gritted his teeth against the memories. Every time Xavier and Elijah would get frustrated with his quick temper, they would tell him to stop acting like Frank.

"Damian, you are a child of God. So was your father. Each with your own free will. Each perfectly designed to love if you have the faith to believe. He had a choice—but so do you."

With a scoff of disbelief, he racked his brain for another topic. The only problem was that his mind wanted to dwell more on the fact that she didn't really know him.

This was more proof that he could never, ever, contemplate a relationship with her.

She liked him now, but she didn't know his dark truths. If she did, she'd put as much distance between them as she could. Just like she had with her sister's boyfriend.

He was too toxic to be in a real relationship. Someone like Lexy deserved a good man who could love her completely. Or at least go to town with her on a dinner date.

Why was he even going there in his brain? He had a job to protect her until she left. That was it. She was a job. Just like his horses. When it was time for them to leave, they left.

The tall grasses swayed around them as they reached the ridge. The ocean spread out before them, the shore reaching north and south as far as the eye could see. Huge slabs of rock tumbled down the side of the cliff into the ocean. The tide was out, so a slip of sand was visible.

Lexy straightened her legs and sat up in the saddle. "Oh, Damian. This is breathtaking. And it's yours."

He shrugged. "It kind of belongs to the foundation now. But you know that. It's amazing how it worked out. The ranch stays together, and the foundation gets to save the nesting area for the turtles. Belle and Quinn make a good team." He had given into the idea of selling part of the ranch to developers. Belle had been trying to keep the ranch working and that had looked to be the only way. He was thankful for Quinn on so many levels. Mainly for Belle's happiness, but for saving the beach too.

He hadn't even realized how much he'd needed it.

She chuckled. "I've been on the shore and under the water, but this is a whole other view here, high on the ridge. I get why you love this land and don't want to leave. I could live right here for the rest of my life and be grateful."

He closed his eyes and allowed the peace that swirled around him to settle. With Lexy, he had started to understand why his brother and cousins spent so much time on the boats and with their families. This land by the sea was the only good thing his father had passed on to his family. Maybe if he focused on the gifts God had given him, he could find happiness.

King tossed his head and shifted his weight. "He's not as impressed as I am." Belle's voices pulled him out of his musings and back to her.

The breeze pulled some of her thick dark hair out of the knot at the base of her neck. Strands waved in front of her face and she tried to tuck them away, but they came back. The sun highlighted her profile. Long lashes fanned out and caught rays of light. Here, high above the endless shore, she was the view that took his breath. King had known from the minute she'd walked into the barn. Damian was a bit slower.

He cleared his throat. "I think he's very impressed. Thank you for stepping in and giving him your time. He needed you."

"Poor baby had some major control issues. He seems so much better. I'm not sure how I helped, but I'm glad he let me."

"He had irrational fears, and I knew it would take time to deal with them. Time I was afraid we didn't have. His newest owner is not that patient." Damian shifted in the saddle. "They've been calling, and I've been ignoring them. Belle should be back soon."

"Fear can keep us from our best life. The one God means for us to have."

Damian turned Rio toward home, and she followed. "Damian, you work so well with traumatized animals because you understand them." King swished his tail and nosed Rio. She nudged him forward so that she and Damian were almost knee to knee. Her leg brushed his. She had bumped the prosthesis. Did she notice?

"Damian?"

He looked up and met her gaze.

Concern filled her eyes. "Are you okay?"

Nodding, he moved ahead to put more distance between them. King easily extended his gait and caught up with them.

"So, what is it?" she asked, in a tone that implied she was repeating herself. "What do you fear?"

His back stiffened and his hands paused on the horse's neck.

"Sorry, that was too personal."

Fear? He feared being his father. He feared the people he loved leaving him. He feared that his father was right and that he was a waste of space. He feared he would fall in love and destroy the woman who trusted him. Just like his father had. Like his brother and cousin almost had with their wives. And he was worse than either of them.

He feared he'd die alone, never having a family of his own. He feared that he already loved Lexy and wouldn't recover when she left. But all he could get out was one word.

"Snakes."

"What?"

"I fear snakes. They're creepy and sneak up on you without warning." He took in a deep breath, letting the fresh scent of ocean and driftwood calm his racing heart. "What about you? What is the fearless Lexy Zapata afraid of?"

"Snakes are not your real—" Her phone vibrated in her back pocket. Naomi's ringtone was muffled behind her denim. "That's my sister." Leaning forward, she pulled King to a stop as she reached for her cell.

She turned to Damian. Fear was stamped on her face.

* * *

Her heart raced as she accepted the call and placed it on the speaker. Why would her sister be calling? "Naomi, What's—"

"There's a truck pulling into the barn area." Her voice was edged in real fear. "I'm hiding with Jessie in the back room. I don't recognize the truck. It's not one from the ranch. I'm scared."

Her gaze stayed focused on Damian. "It's okay. We aren't that far."

Damian had already moved Rio into a faster pace. "Naomi, keep the door locked and stay quiet. Make sure to silence your phone. We aren't far from you," he reassured them.

"Okay." Her sister disconnected.

The pit of Lexy's stomach cramped. "She sounded so scared." And she wasn't there to protect her sister and niece.

"Stay calm. King'll get tense if you do."

Taking a deep breath and rubbing the horse's neck, she leaned forward. "Get us home, boy. I shouldn't have left her alone." She could hear the stupid tears in her voice.

"You didn't leave. We are a few minutes away."

"Do you know what an angry man can do in that amount of time?"

"Yes. Lexy, the best thing you can do for your sister is to stay calm. How fast do you think you can take him?"

"You go as fast as you can, and we'll follow. Don't worry about me."

With a nod, he clicked his tongue and Rio lunged. King's ears perked and his muscles bunched. "You want to go?" She slid the reins up his neck and pressed her heels into his side. His legs stretched and they were galloping down the path.

She stayed low as they ran alongside Damian and Rio. Her heart was beating faster than King's hooves pounding the soft dirt. Damian held up his hand for her to slow.

For the first second, King fought her for control, then he slowed to a canter. The cabins came into view. "Do you recognize the truck?" There was someone inside the cab. Hopefully it's just the one person.

Now at a slow walk, the horse snorted and breathed hard. Damian stayed low over his horse. "Stay here and I'll go around to the back of the barn."

As Rio crossed in front of her, the truck door opened. A tall man jumped down from the high seat. *Beckett.* "It's Beckett." Lexy's body sagged, almost collapsing in relief. She pulled out her phone and texted her sister.

"It's not Steve or the men looking for him. It's Beckett," she said to Damian, like he couldn't see who was standing in front of his barn.

"I see that." He pulled Rio next to her and they walked side by side to the barn. Damian and Rio acted casual and unfazed, not as if they had just been running for their lives. Or the lives of her sister and niece.

"Beckett!" She waved wildly.

The teenager turned, then smiled when he saw them.

"You're by yourself?" Damian asked the teen, giving Lexy time to catch her breath. "We were coming to town today to pick up the supplies."

The boy's brows went up. "You were coming into town?" With an obvious shock, Beckett turned to Lexy.

"He's coming into town. Port Del Mar?" He whispered to Lexy as if Damian wasn't standing there.

"Yep," she answered. King shifted his weight, still restless from the run. Swinging her leg over the saddle, she dismounted and scratched his jaw. "He's *driving* to town, but don't count on him getting out of the truck. Yet." She grinned and winked at Damian. "One baby step at a time."

"There is absolutely no reason for me to get out of the truck, and there is nothing baby about me." He dismounted from the right side, then paused to ensure he had his balance before slipping his boot out of the stirrup. He followed that with a disgruntled look directed at Lexy.

Beckett stared at them wide-eyed, then cleared his throat. "I'll start unloading while you rub down the horses."

Damian shook his head. "Lexy needs to check on her sister. Will you take Rio, Beckett?"

The young man straightened, and a huge smile lit his face. "Yes, sir. I can help with the horses."

Lexy hugged him. "Thank you."

Damian handed the reins to the teen and took King from her. "So, what really brought you out here?" His tone was slightly aggressive.

Lexy was about to tell him to be nice, but Beckett looked straight at him and lifted his chin. There was a slight tremble in his stance. "I need you to teach me how to dance."

For a moment Lexy was unable to move. She held her breath.

Damian's brows pulled in as if he'd spoken a different language. He glanced at Lexy. She took a step toward them. But he shook his head and lifted his chin to the cabin. He was right. She needed to go to her sister.

He turned back to Beckett. "Let's take care of the horses and unload the supplies. Lexy will be back soon and you can talk to her."

"But…" the boy started, then glanced over his shoulder. "Okay."

Damian was already halfway to the barn. Lexy gave the boy a nod, then turned to the cabins. Her sister needed her right now. She'd have to trust Damian not to damage Beckett's fragile confidence. She had told him he was a good man. Did she believe it?

Taking the steps two at a time, she realized she did. He might not trust himself, but he'd be careful. He wouldn't hurt him.

She grinned. Beckett wanted Damian to teach him to dance. That was going to be fun.

Chapter Twelve

At Damian's tap to his fetlock, King offered his hoof to be checked. It had been a few weeks since the farrier had been out. Belle usually scheduled the appointments. Did he need to contact Brody? He sighed. Getting Brody out to trim the horses should be his responsibility anyway. A few of the horses needed to be shod. It was time to stop acting like a pouting toddler.

More people to deal with. Going to the next hoof, he bit down hard on his back teeth. Had Belle left him on purpose to force him out of hermit mode?

Standing, he ran his hand along King's back. "Like the world revolves around me. Belle deserves to travel and spend time with her family. Have I always been this self-centered?"

The question was met with silence. "Okay. First on my to-do list is to call Brody." He tossed the pick into the caddy. "There are probably a number of people I need to call."

"Mr. De La Rosa?" Beckett stood in the barn door with Rio. "He's done."

"Your mom let you drive out here alone?" He didn't

want to have anything to do with dancing or helping a teenage boy. Leading King to the paddock, he glanced over at Lexy's cabin. How long would it take her to calm her sister down?

Maybe something was wrong. "Rio needs to be turned out to pasture." He pointed to the other door.

The boy petted the roan's muzzle. "I can do it. Thank you for letting me stay." He looked at his phone, then glanced at him. There was a nervousness about him.

"Turn Rio out. Then we'll talk."

"Yes, sir." He paused as if to say something else, then turned back to the horse. Damian went to unload the truck, still thinking about Lexy. Maybe he should go check on them. He picked up a feed bag instead.

Beckett joined him, lifting another feed sack and following him to the barn. His phone went off as he placed the bag on the floor. He glanced at it, then declined the call. "Will you help me with dancing? I might not have much time left."

Damian narrowed his eyes. "Does your mother know you drove out here alone?"

He rolled his eyes and shrugged. "I used to do deliveries for the store all the time."

"That was before. Beckett, does she know you're here?"

"It's not fair that my life has been turned into a before and after. I want to do all the things I did before. I want to…to be me again." His eyes glistened with moisture.

Oh, no. No. No. Damian's gaze darted to the door. Lexy needed to get here now. There was nothing about him that was equipped to handle an emotional teenage boy.

The loudest sigh he'd ever heard filled the barn. "Sorry. I just get frustrated and the word *before* sets me off."

"Consider the word struck from my vocabulary." His muscles eased as the crisis was diverted.

"Will you please help me before she finds out and hauls me back to the house and grounds me till I'm forty? I have a winter social and I want to ask Tory, but I haven't tried dancing since I lost my leg. I don't want to fall or look like an idiot. Everyone will be staring at me as it is, and I don't want to make it worse."

He gritted his teeth. Yep, he'd relaxed too soon. "You can't lie to your mom."

The boy's eyes teared up again and his jaw flexed as if he was battling all the emotions brewing in his eyes. Damian groaned.

Don't back down. Don't give in.

Rubbing the back of his neck, Damian stretched it left, then right. He had to avoid the kid's eyes, or he would go all soft. He looked at the heavy beams overhead. "Call her or get off my property now."

"But, Mr. De La Rosa." Desperation cut through his voice.

Lexy came through the barn door just in time to hear Damian's last statement. Wrapping her arm around Beckett, she glared at him. He closed his eyes and rubbed the bridge of his nose.

"Damian De La Rosa." The crisp, disapproving tone was a perfect blend of his mother and the school librarian. Growing up as a boy who loved the outdoors but was forced to sit in a classroom, he had been all too familiar with it.

Beckett stood straight in the shelter of Lexy's arm.

"There is absolutely no reason to threaten and scare the boy." Her glare would've turned him to ash if he'd been a weaker man.

He pointed at the six-foot *boy*. "Your protégé stole his family's truck and drove out here without telling anyone. My guess is that his mother is worried. If he wants my help, he will call his mother right now."

"I didn't steal the truck." Anger pierced each word. But the moisture that he blinked back in his eyes told another story. "I knew she wouldn't let me come. This is Tory's last year, then she's leaving for college." He looked down at Lexy, his eyes big and pleading. "Mom's already said I need to stay close for college. Tory's going to Lubbock. That's so far away, and I'll be stuck here. I just want to dance with her before she leaves."

Lexy hugged the teen closer. "I know. But Damian's right. You can't run off like that. How can your mother trust you with bigger choices? Call her and I'll explain things."

"What makes y'all think I know anything about dancing?" He frowned at them.

"You do so much. Riding, diving, you have such good balance."

He wasn't going to do this. "You have a physical therapist. Go to them. They're trained for this kind of thing."

"I don't see them as much now. Plus, Mom and Dad were talking about the money my legs cost. It's too much. If I ask to go, it'll be extra. You can do it for free. I'll work for you or whatever you want. And I want you to help me because you get it. The therapist is great and all. But you know what it feels like to have people stare at you. The best ways to avoid falling. You get it. Please, just give me enough tips so I won't embarrass Tory."

"If she's embarrassed by you, then she's not worth your time and effort." He slipped past them to unload the rest of the supplies. The boy had asked for his help. That was tough to ignore. "Call your mom. Then we'll talk."

"Yes, sir." He had his phone to his ear before Damian stopped talking.

Now, with the last of the delivery unloaded, Damian stood in the doorway with his hand on his hip. Hansel nosed his fingers and gave him a soft whine.

"Yeah, I'm not sure how to handle all these people in our space either." He moved to his front porch to wait for Mrs. Keller's verdict. Damian eased into the rocking chair and for the first time, picked up the Bible Elijah had left a few months back. His family thought he didn't know they took turns to do their secret wellness checks. They weren't so secret.

He resented them and did everything he could think of to chase them off, but they kept coming back. A hard knot lodged itself in the center of his chest. They loved him—and kept loving him, despite the hateful ways he treated them.

Why had they not given up on him? There was nothing he had done to deserve them or their faith in him.

He flipped through the pages of the Bible. The spine was stiff from lack of use. Elijah had marked several pages. Damian stopped and read verse 2 Corinthians 5:17:

Therefore, if any man is in Christ, he is a new creature: old things are passed away; behold, all things have become new.

A smile pulled at the corner of his lips. Elijah wasn't even trying to be subtle. They had been raised by Frank De La Rosa. The whole county knew what kind of man he was, and godly was not anywhere on the list. Elijah knew and understood his fears of being like his father.

Elijah and Xavier had grown out of Frank's drunken, abusive shadow. It hadn't been easy for them and they had hurt the women in their lives—strong women who had forgiven them.

He wasn't sure they deserved a second chance. But they had always been better men than his father. And the steadfast love of their wives, Jazz and Selena, had proved that.

Was he a better man than Frank? For most of his life, he'd heard how much he was like his father. Had there ever been anything good about the man? Did he carry Frank's mean, abusive personality in his DNA? Or was he using his father as an excuse to hide from life?

Looking up from the Bible, he scanned the area. Lexy stood outside King's paddock with the phone to her ear, talking to Beckett's mother. The horse played with her braid, and she caressed his neck.

She jumped into people's lives without thought of being hurt. What if he let her into his life? His heart.

Who was he kidding? He'd seen his mother's face when his father had lost control. The shadows in his cousins' eyes when thunderstorms brought back the worst childhood memories. Belle, cowering in the old dirty shed, hungry and scared.

He couldn't risk being the monster in someone else's dreams.

Lexy walked back into the barn. A few minutes later,

Beckett ran up his driveway, his uneven gait noticeable in his excitement.

"Mr. De La Rosa! My mother has given me one hour. So, where do you want to dance? In the barn or your cabin?"

Lexy followed, grinning. "She doesn't want him to overdo it or to bother you for too long." She looked at Beckett. "Agreed, right?"

"Yes, ma'am. I have my alarm set."

He sighed. There was no way out of this without hurting anyone's feelings. "Behind the barn." The whole idea of how others felt was a bit new. It had to be Lexy's fault. "I've got a sound system and smooth ground back there."

Lexy took Beckett's hand. "Any special song?"

"Tory and I used to two-step. Anything by George Strait would work." He looked at Damian. "What do you think?"

He almost laughed. *Now* they wanted to know what he thought. "I can't guarantee you won't fall. When you take this kind of risk, you have to be willing to deal with failure."

"See, this is why I want you to teach me. My hope is that, the more I fall here, the better prepared I'll be with Tory. It's so frustrating, relearning something you already know how to do. They say falling is part of learning, but it would be the worst for it to happen front of all my classmates. Someone would probably take a video. Mainly I don't want Tory to be embarrassed or hurt."

He gritted his teeth. The boy was protecting his girl and his pride from losers. If he'd give him the names of anyone that hurt him, he'd… He sighed. Caring about people was hard because there was no way to protect them. "Those people don't matter. We'll do this."

"Damian. Thank you." There was evidence of moisture in his dark eyes.

"Nope." He held up a finger. "If we are going to do this, no tears."

"Right." The teen smiled and his eyes cleared. He turned and headed to the barn.

Lexy took his hand and pulled him along as she followed the teen. The touch didn't mean anything other than to make sure he didn't escape. But he wanted to tighten his grip and never let go, even though that wouldn't be fair to her.

Beckett stopped in the middle of the slab and turned. "You've helped me in more ways than you'll ever know. I just want you to know that, even before you knew who I was, you made an impact on my life."

He swallowed the lump that had formed in his throat. It was too close to the scripture his mom had loved: "Before I formed you in the womb, I knew you."

She would tell them that with God there were no mistakes. Since Thanksgiving, he kept hearing God's words everywhere. Had it been Lexy's prayer or Elijah's Bible… or was he just listening more than he had been before?

He looked to Lexy. "Do you have music?"

"Yes, I do." She held up her phone and smiled. Of course she did. They were pushing him to do things he'd avoided for years. Her eyes bright with delighted mischief. He realized that one of the reasons he was doing this was to see her smile. He'd do just about anything to give her that kind of happiness.

He wanted it to be her he was dancing with. He closed his eyes and erased that thought from his brain.

Beckett had asked for his help and he was going to give it.

There would be no dancing with Lexy Zapata tonight, or in the future. He turned to Beckett and tried not to scowl at him. Less than an hour. He could do this.

"How about 'Baby Blue'? It's the first song that came up." She connected her phone to Damian's sound system. He didn't seem to be paying attention. She waved at him. "Hey! 'Baby Blue' work for you?"

"If it works for him."

Beckett nodded and held out his right hand. When Damian lifted his short arm, he smiled. The slow country ballad played.

"You do realize dancing with Tory has advantages over dancing with me. She's shorter and has both hands."

Beckett laughed and placed his hand high on Damian's back. Damian shook his head.

"Move your hand to my lower ribs. It'll level your shoulders and make it easier to keep your balance."

They were so focused on the best way to move that Lexy thought she could probably leave and they wouldn't notice. She moved to the barn door but stopped when Damian gave her a panicked look. She went back to the upturned bucket and sat down. The man had faced gunfire, explosions and horses no one else could ride, but leave him alone with a teenager and he turned into a big baby.

He used the same even tone and patience with Beckett that he used with the horses. How could the world see him as mean and distant? Under all those scowls and growls, he had to be the kindest man she knew.

After a few missteps, he leaned back. "Do you need to rest, or are you ready to try dancing through a song?"

"Let's dance."

Lexy hit Replay and was amazed as Damian adapted movements for Beckett. At first, they were stiff, but she saw the boy start to relax and laugh at his own missteps.

Damian stopped. "You should dance with Lexy. It would be more like dancing with Tory." Beckett got all nervous again.

"It's all right," Lexy said. "I haven't danced in so long I'll probably step on your toes."

Beckett grinned. "Fifty-fifty chance I won't feel it." They moved around the area, the music filling the air. She made eye contact with Damian and he smiled at her.

Then Beckett's body turned but his leg didn't, and he lost his balance and fell backward. He let go of Lexy, so she wouldn't go down with him.

Damian grinned and held out his hand. "First fall and the earth didn't split open?"

"And you looked graceful doing it, too," Lexy added.

The kid stood. "That wasn't too bad."

"The problem with some therapy is that it focuses on linear motion." Damian stood beside Beckett as he demonstrated a movement. "Dancing requires a lot of single-stance activities and lateral movements that aren't part of standard therapy programs."

Beckett nodded. "You should be a therapist."

He laughed wholeheartedly. It was the first time Lexy had seen him laugh with such gusto. "People skills might be a requirement."

Was he lying to himself, or were there other issues she couldn't see?

He showed Beckett how to use his core, hip and other

leg to create motion, then guided him through the movements as they went through the dance again. Their legs tangled and they both went down. Lexy jumped from her bucket to help, but they didn't need her. They were up and at it again in a moment.

"You could add this move to it." Damian pivoted on his right leg, lifting the boy slightly so that he spun.

"Oh, that was so cool." The joy in the Beckett's face nearly brought Lexy to tears. The simple act of dance that everyone else took for granted was a gift that Damian was giving him.

How could she not fall in love with this man?

Love?

She stood, her hands in white-knuckled fists. She was not in love with him. She wasn't. It was... It was just the music and watching them dance. And seeing him with the horses and the baby and diving with her.

No. She couldn't fall in love with him. That had disaster written all over it.

"Lexy?" The music had stopped. Beckett was studying her, concern in his face. She had to leave before she broke down. "Yes. I just remembered something. Never mind me." It came out in a high-pitched Irish accent. "It can wait. I just...uhm...want to write it down. I'll be right back."

Ducking into the barn, she leaned against the wall. They continued practicing outside. Even the sound of his voice drew her in. She could just stand here and listen to him.

"To make this work, you need to practice with Tory and show her what you need in order to dance. Would she do that?"

They continued talking and she got her breathing and

her heart rate back under control. Loving him didn't change anything, so she was just going to let it pass. She'd put it on a cloud and let it float away. *Dear God, please guide me and help me keep my focus on what needs to be done.*

One more cleansing breath and she joined them outside. "Amarillo by Morning" was playing now.

She was so proud of both of them. How had they become so important to her in just a few weeks? "Beckett, you look great."

"Thanks." He was looking down at his feet. "I just don't want to have people laughing at us."

Damian put a hand on Hansel but focused his attention on Beckett. "I know this is easier said than done, but you can't worry about what others think. If you do, you'll stop living. And life is too wonderful to give up."

Beckett nodded. "I know I kind of forced myself on you. Thank you, Mr. De La Rosa. You don't know what it has meant to me just to be around you. You've inspired me in so many ways. I just want life to go back to normal. I want it to be like it was before."

Damian tilted his head and twisted his mouth. "That's a pointless wish. Life changes us. We never stay the same."

"That's so true," Lexy agreed. She wanted to pull them both into a tight hug. She settled for adjusting the strings of Beckett's hoodie instead. "We get older. You'll graduate. People will come and go from your life. And each one will bring something new or take a piece of your heart with them. Some by choice, others through death. Sometimes we get to plan change, and that can be exciting. But a lot of the time, we don't."

Beckett nodded. "Like going away to school, taking

a job far away." He looked at Damian. "But you seem to do the same things."

He rubbed his left arm. "I'm not the same, though. The military alone changed me. You can grow and adapt or become angry and bitter. Your choice."

Beckett gave him a half smile. "Or we can isolate ourselves from the world."

He narrowed his eyes. "That hits a little too close."

Beckett's laugh was interrupted by the alarm on his phone. "Oh, no. Not already." He looked at the phone, and his shoulders slumped. "I've got to go. Thanks again. Just promise me one thing."

Damian raised his eyebrows.

Beckett grinned as he climbed into his truck. "Promise you'll dance with Lexy."

Damian looked a little lost as he watched Beckett drive away. He scanned the horizon, looking for an escape.

"It's okay. You don't have to dance with me."

The playlist looped back to the first song, "Baby Blue." Damian closed his eyes and sang along. He sang about a woman who added color to his life before she left. He lifted his hand to her, palm up.

Unable to resist, her fingers reached for him. His hand went to her waist and her hand rested on his left shoulder. They didn't cover much space, just swaying as the song played. His breath gently caressed her cheek as he sang. The words were low, as if he were speaking to himself.

She wanted to rest her head on his shoulder and block out the world. Instead, she made sure to keep a safe distance between them. He continued to sing about a man who couldn't stop dreaming of a woman who left him. When the playlist moved on to the next song, he stopped. His hand went to her jaw. Her heart rate jumped.

He was going to kiss her. She lifted her face to his, but he didn't move. He just stared at her, his warm fingers gently gripping her skin. "Damian?"

"Shhh." His hand moved to her neck. The warmth seeped into her, making her feel cherished. "You're so beautiful and amazing. Why are you single?"

"You're such a nice guy. Why do you hide it?"

He gave her a lopsided grin. "I'm not. You just see something that's not there."

"Are you going to kiss me or just stare at me?"

He moved down. Her mouth went dry. Finally, their lips made contact. She allowed the world to slip away and she focused on everything he was making her feel. She reached up and circled her arms around his neck. Her fingers slipped through his hair. It was thick, but so soft.

In his arms, the problems that tossed her in a storm disappeared. This connection to Damian anchored her.

She knew that, no matter how rough the storm, he would shelter her. His kisses moved from her mouth to the corner of her eye to her forehead. He stopped there. With his lips pressed against her skin, they both were out of breath. Her hands dropped to his shoulders.

The desire to stay in his arms overrode all her common sense. Closing her eyes, she battled her heartbeat back into submission.

His fingers flexed, then dropped away as he stepped back from her.

Looking up she studied his face. "You are an unexpected change to my life, Mr. De La Rosa. It's safe to say I'll never be the same." It was too early to know whether it was a good or bad change.

"You too, Lexy Zapata." His Spanish-moss eyes were full of an emotion she couldn't pinpoint.

"If I had the option to stay, could there be something more between us?" She had to ask.

Say yes. Please say yes. His gaze searched hers. She stopped breathing. He pulled his lips into a thin line, then looked down. Chin back up, regret cloaked his features.

She tried to laugh, to stop him from saying the words she didn't want to hear. It probably sounded more like glass in a disposal. "Never mind. I don't even know why I asked. I have to make sure my sister and niece are safe. After what happened this last year, they'll come first from now on."

She wrapped her arms around her middle. Had the temperature suddenly dropped? "I love my work and that means traveling. That's been my dream for so long and now I have these incredible opportunities. Staying here is not an option."

He hadn't said a word, just stood there all stoic as she fell apart. Behind him were the barns and the cabins, all surrounded by the vast family ranch. This was where he belonged.

The part of her brain that was ruled by her heart wanted to grab hold of him and ask him to let her belong too.

But her rational brain knew the truth. There were no happy endings. The ranch represented freedom now, but it would become its own trap that would lead them to regret. She had plans and a family to protect. He wanted to be alone.

He shifted his weight, but his gaze stayed trained on her. "Lexy." His full lips pulled at the corners and he acted as if he had something to say to all her nonsense.

Maybe he did understand and could explain all this to her.

He sighed. "Not many people get the opportunity to catch the dream they've been chasing. Your leaving is for the best. I'm tired and need to go in. See you tomorrow."

She didn't want him to leave her. Not yet. "Come over for dinner."

He shook his head. "It's been a long day. I need to take my leg off and get some rest." And with that, he turned away from her.

He left her standing alone. Why did she want to cry? He was right, this was for the best.

Chapter Thirteen

Damian sat on his porch drinking his coffee and flipping through the Bible Elijah had left months ago. Unexpectedly, reading had become a welcomed part of his morning routine. The cabin next door opened. His favorite little family made their way to the back where Lexy hid her car.

He frowned. Where were they going so early Sunday morning? Gretel trotted over and settled in next to Hansel. "So where are our ladies going?"

She thumped her tail and looked at him as if she knew all the secrets but wouldn't snitch. He thought about calling her several times, but after their kiss yesterday he thought it best to give Lexy space.

She had talked about staying. He had wanted to grab her and say yes. If she stayed, he'd...what? Love her until she hated him.

The Bible said he could be a new creature. But how could he guarantee that his father's DNA wouldn't raise its head and strike.

Cup empty, he set the Bible on the table and went

to the barns. The dogs ran ahead, playing tug-of-war with an old toy.

He went to the feed room and prepped the horses' morning meals. Lexy and Naomi never left this early for church.

They couldn't be leaving for good. They would have said goodbye. Maybe. The Christmas lights would go out and no one would be there to turn them on. Dreary gray would cover his world in loneliness again. He hadn't minded before, but now he knew the difference.

He went to the last stall of the morning. King came to him and nudged his chest. "She got you, too, didn't she? I don't think either of us will ever be the same." Even with the huge strides the horse had made, he'd never be the show performer his owners were expecting.

With his deep psychological scars, a crowded, noisy event would be too much for him to handle. "She was right. We are too much alike. Not much good for anyone."

A vehicle approached the barns. Damian scowled as he went to the doors. Did he need to be armed?

It was Belle.

"Sorry about showing up unannounced. I tried to call, but you didn't answer."

He patted his pocket. "Must have left my phone on the porch. When did you get back?"

"Last night." Belle smiled.

"And you couldn't wait to check on me." He stood and headed to the barn.

Belle followed, then slightly leaned into his side and watched King run.

"Looks like things are going well here."

He gave her a sideways glance. She had a look about

her...determined. He didn't know what was coming, but he was pretty sure he didn't want to hear it.

"Damian. I know your tricks. You can stay silent all you want, but I'm not going anywhere. I'll call your list of clients this afternoon."

"I've already contacted them. My clients aren't your responsibility. I'll give reports and let them know when the horses are ready. Sorry it's taken me so long to step up and do that part of my job."

"Wow. Jazz and Selena were right."

He wanted to groan. If the women of his family were talking about him, it couldn't be good. It never was. He was afraid, deeply afraid, so he didn't take the bait.

"Don't you want to know?" she asked.

He shrugged.

She looked toward his cabin. "Christmas decorations, hmm?"

"Against my will."

She snorted. "I've never known you to do anything you didn't want to do. I hear you've been driving into town every morning. And scuba diving with Lexy?"

"There were issues with a violent ex and Lexy needed a buddy to dive."

"And you've been mentoring the Keller boy."

He gave up. "What's your point?"

She leaned in closer. "The sisters-in-law say you're in love with Lexy Zapata."

The best course of action was to remain silent and pretend he was clueless to anything she was saying. The more he'd tried to explain, the worse it would sound.

"It has to be love."

"No. Shouldn't you be going to church?"

She turned to face him, her hand on his arm. "Damian, not long ago you told me we didn't deserve Frank's treatment of us. You said I deserve to be loved. You were right." Her gaze went to the horizon, then back to him.

"I can't even imagine settling back into normal life after facing war and the loss of your limbs. But you are not alone. Xavier has a group he meets with that have helped him adjust back into a normal life. Elijah has used counseling and groups to deal with the issues in his head. I know you don't drink, but I want you to know, there are people who understand and can help."

He tilted his chin to the sky and looked at the clouds. Belle didn't go anywhere. She stood there and waited for him to reply. Like a normal conversation.

"This isn't about the war or my injuries." He jabbed his finger against his forehead. "Frank is in here."

"What? No." Horror filled her face. "You are nothing like your father. How can you even think that?"

"Even my mother said I was just like my father when I threw a fit. She told me to stop acting like him. And Xavier and Elijah—all the time."

Her fingers tightened around his arm. "Damian, look at me." He didn't. "You look the most like Frank and you have the same skill he had with horses, but those are the *good* things about him. You've never been mean or violent. You're a hero."

"I am not a hero." He forced the words out between gritted teeth. "I didn't join the army as a great patriotic sacrifice. I hated my father and wanted to get as far away from him as I could. He told me not to join. I lost my temper. We got in a fight—a physical fight. I get so angry sometimes. I hate being around people. Everyone in town thinks I'm just like him."

"Then they don't know you. You get angry?" She clicked her tongue and shook her head. "I can tell you stories about my anger. We have every right to be angry about our childhood. But what do you do when you're angry? Have you ever hurt anyone? Other than Frank."

He scowled. Needing distance, he moved away from her. "I feel this darkness that sits on my chest. I know it's that thing that turned Frank into a mean drunk. It's in me."

She reached for him, looking suspiciously as if she was going in for a hug. Why was she so convinced he wasn't the monster Frank was?

"This is the reason you won't do anything about your feelings for Lexy?" She stayed right next to him as he walked toward his cabin.

"Damian! Don't self-sabotage. Believe me, I've been there, done that—and you're the one who talked me off the ledge. Maybe the thing between you and Lexy won't work. But give yourself permission to find out. There's a good chance she needs to be loved by you as much as you need her love."

"I'm so messed up. Why would she want to have anything to do with me? She deserves better than some cowboy with hidden monsters. I told you, I'm broken. And before you get all upset, I'm not talking about my body." He pressed his knuckles against his heartbeat. "I'm not sure I have enough here to give her."

"Don't cut her out of your life without giving it a chance." Her warm fingers squeezed his arm. She didn't allow him to get away from her this time. Her gaze pierced him. The moisture tore at his gut. Disappointing her was the last thing he wanted to do, but he didn't know how to be the man she thought he was.

"Damian. Don't you understand. You might be the

perfect man for her—broken bits and all. Perfection is so overrated. When you love you love deeply and completely. Damian, I've seen it. You never give up, and she needs that. She needs you."

"But Frank is right here." He pointed to his head. "What if he takes over? Just once would be one time too many."

"Frank made choices that deeply hurt other people, and that's no one's fault but his own. He left scars. I struggled with letting Quinn love me. You know what I found out?"

He looked at her. "That you're an incredible woman and mother who deserves to be loved wholeheartedly?"

"Well, there is that. But Quinn needed to love me as much as I needed to let him love me. I love that man more than I thought possible. With the right person, love is a two-way gift. To love and be loved. We all deserve that. God loves you and… And Lexy Zapata deserves to be loved by you. You're an incredible man, Damian De La Rosa."

"She's leaving the country."

"A temporary job for the foundation. She could come back here. Her job includes sites all over the world, but she'll need a home base. Why can't this be hers?"

He yanked his hat lower over his eyes. His head hurt. If he could just make it inside the cabin, maybe she'd leave. He put his foot on the bottom step.

She sighed. "I know. We've talked more this morning than we have in the last three years combined. I'll let you go. We're leaving for church soon. Today is all about Christmas music. You should think about joining us. Your mom always sang in the choir. You did too."

She kissed his cheek. "I love you, Damian. Growing

up, you stood between Frank and me more times than I can count. Please don't lock that boy away because you're afraid of something that's not even there. Come to the Christmas service today and worship with us."

"I don't go to town."

"I hear you have."

"I drove into town, but I didn't get out of the truck or talk to anyone. I'm not going to church."

"Not even for her?" With a smile, she turned to her truck and nearly skipped to their car. He thought of the girl she had been and the happiness she had now. Was she right? Could he love someone without the darkness slipping past his walls?

On the table, the Bible was open to Philippians. Elijah had highlighted a verse in blue. "I can do all things through Christ which strengthened me." In the margin, he had written: *Can't do this alone.*

Damian dropped into the chair, his shoulders heavy. *God, can I truly be a man worthy of a woman like Lexy?*

Holding the Bible, he bowed in prayer. *Dear Lord, I turn all my worry and guilt over. Please take them from me.*

In silence, he waited. For what, he wasn't sure. All around him, nature continued to move and thrive. He closed his eyes and tried again. It had been so long since he'd prayed. Maybe he wasn't doing it right.

Opening his eyes, he took in the land around him, the beauty that surrounded this edge of the world he got to call home. This ranch was his sanctuary. A gift from God that he had taken for granted, just like he did the support and love of his brother and cousins.

Before he could think about having any other relationship, he needed to work on repairing his one with God.

* * *

Lexy didn't need the hymnal to sing along with "God Rest Ye Merry Gentlemen." She found such warmth and comfort in the traditional songs of Christmas. Red poinsettias covered the church. Naomi was in the front row of the choir. It was so nice to hear her strong, sweet voice blending with the others.

She sat behind half of the De La Rosa family. The other half were in the choir with her sister. Leaving was going to be hard.

The pastor stood and opened his Bible. In the choir, Naomi's eyes went wide, and she elbowed Selena, who was standing next to her. The other woman's face showed the same shocked look, then relaxed into a warm smile. Twisting to her left, Lexy felt the air stop moving to her lungs.

Damian was walking down the aisle. Black hat in hand, he made eye contact with her. He stopped at her pew.

"Can I sit here?" he whispered.

"Yes." She scooted over to give him room.

"Sorry, I'm late." There was a slight shake to his strong hand, but he looked straight ahead as if being in church was a normal part of his Sunday.

"You're good. Only missed one song."

Her mind was reeling. Damian had come to church and was sitting next to her. Elijah, sitting directly in front of them, gave him a low thumbs-up, but didn't turn around. Xavier glanced over his shoulder with a quick nod.

There was a noise at the back of the church, and everyone turned to look at the group of small shepherds gathered there. Belle's youngest daughter gasped and ran to Damian. She threw her arms around him. There was a smattering of chuckles. "Tío Damian! I told Cassie you'd be here, but she said don't hold my breath. But I prayed and asked God."

He kissed her forehead. "I'm here and you should be there." He pointed to the other little shepherds waiting for her.

With a giggle, she joined the others.

Pastor Rodriguez read from the Bible. "And there were in the same country shepherds abiding in the field, keeping watch over their flock by night." Some of the little shepherds waved their floppy toy sheep.

The pastor continued. "And, lo, the angel of the Lord came upon them, and the glory of the Lord shone round about them…" From the side entrance, twelve older children wearing wings and robes joined the choir in singing "Hark! The Herald Angels Sing." The words and music vibrated in Lexy's heart as Damian sang along under his breath.

Selena stepped forward. "And the angel said unto them, Fear not: for, behold, I bring you good tidings of great joy, which shall be to all people. For unto you is born this day in the city of David a Savior, which is Christ the Lord."

Voices lifted as one in "It Came Upon the Midnight Clear." Lexy's heart swelled as she watched her sister among their new friends.

Naomi was next to read from the Bible. "And they came with haste, and found Mary, and Joseph and the babe lying in a manger."

Damian leaned into her and gave her a half grin. A weightless fluttering tugged at her stomach. Had her sister read that passage on purpose?

A couple of teens dressed as the holy family came down the far-right aisle, walking alongside the windows. The colors from the stained-glass windows washed across the pews and the choir continued with "O Little Town of Bethlehem."

The pastor read again. "But Mary kept all these things and pondered them in her heart."

Lexy choked back the hard knot in her throat. Her mother would have loved this.

With her last words, her mother had told her to find joy in life. Was that here in Port Del Mar? Or was her future somewhere out in the world?

She glanced up at Damian, then whispered, "Your mother would be proud of you. Not for being here, but for all the good you do. You're a shepherd and innkeeper rolled into one."

His jaw hardened and his Adam's apple moved up and down, as if he were trying to swallow but couldn't. He dropped his head and closed his eyes, but not before she saw the emotion in them. Why had she said that? And why now?

"I'm sorry." She hadn't meant to upset him.

His hand reached for hers. Fingers intertwined, she tightened her grip to reassure him. The words of "The First Noel" came up on the screen and the congregation stood to sing.

With the last song sung, the pastor asked everyone to join hands. As people reached crossed the aisle, Damian looked uncomfortable. Lexy started to switch sides, so she'd be on Damian's left side, but Beckett beat her to it. Stepping into the aisle, the boy wrapped his hand around his bicep. Heads bowed, they prayed.

She took a deep breath and focused on God's deep

and forever love. The pastor spoke of the holy family seeking shelter deep into the night. He finished with reminding them to all seek the shelter God offers in His Word. "He is there even during the coldest winters of life."

Silently, Lexy added her own thanks for the safe harbor God had put in their path so many weeks ago. *God, do You mean for us to stay here, or is this a temporary shelter?*

Would his mother be proud of him? He was so far from the boy she'd loved. He'd grown up in this church. Sitting with his mother, singing in the choir, helping serve dinners and even playing Joseph. Lexy's whispered words had hit him hard.

Damian kept his head down as he poured out his thanks to God. The horses that came to him fearful and wounded. Their healing gave his life purpose. He realized now that they were his group therapy. They gave him so much more than they received from him.

The pastor ended the prayer, but Damian wanted to stay. He wanted to go to his knees and beg God for forgiveness. He'd allowed everything his mother had taught him to go to waste because of his hatred for his father. Frank had lived in hatred, turning his back on love and forgiveness.

Around him, people began to move. Lexy squeezed his hand and then let go.

Beckett turned and hugged him. "Wow, man. So cool to see you here." He leaned in and whispered, "Tory and I are practicing dancing. She thought it was a great idea." With satisfaction on his face, he stepped back.

"She wanted to ask me but didn't know if it would make me feel bad. Thank you."

Damian gave the boy's shoulder a quick squeeze. "Happy to hear it."

Beckett's parents greeted him. Mrs. Keller went in for a hug and didn't let go. "You've done more than I can thank you for. Not only for Beckett, but for the whole family." She leaned back but her hands stayed on his biceps. "You have a special gift for healing hurts in animals and people. Thank you." One more hug and she followed her family out.

His nerves were raw. Others stopped to greet him and shake his hand. He flexed his shoulder, trying to relax. He'd forgotten this part.

When he decided to attend the Christmas service, he thought the walking in would be the hardest thing. It hadn't occurred to him to have an exit plan in place. A wall of people milled around him, standing between him and the door. He couldn't breathe.

Okay, God. You got me here. Now please give me a way out.

There was a gentle surge as his family surrounded him, smiling and talking to people as they cleared a subtle path to the side door. Love just about popped his heart. A hand slipped around his arm. Lexy was next to him, guiding him out.

The air outside was fresh and cool. "The family goes to the Painted Dolphin." She grinned. "Do you want to go?"

His first full breath of air ended in a laugh. "Ahh, no. I have hit my limit of social interaction for today. Maybe next week. But you go."

Naomi was on his other side. "I would love to go

home and relax. How about you ride with Damian, and I'll pick up something to go. We can have a quiet lunch at the cabins."

With a quick glance his way, Lexy replied. "I love that idea. But you should go on home with Jess. Damian can drive me over to pick up lunch. We'll be right behind you." She looked at him again. "That okay with you?"

"Good, but we need to go before the family finds us."

They made sure Naomi and Jess were secure and on the road, then went to pick up the order Lexy placed at the Painted Dolphin.

In less than twenty minutes, they were pulling up to the cabin with the cab of the truck full of fajitas and fresh tortillas, along with half of a fragrant blackberry cobbler.

As they climbed out of the truck, a muffled cry came from behind her cabin. "Steve, no!"

"Get out of the car," a harsh male voice tinged with anger yelled.

Damian stepped in front of Lexy and held up his hand for her to be still.

"That's Naomi." She tried to dart in front of him. He caught her arm.

"Shhh."

With his hand on her arm, he moved slowly to the side of her cabin.

"Let me—" Naomi's words were cut off.

"Shut up and just come with me." The angry male voice was harsh. "We need to talk."

Lexy tried to lunge forward again, but Damian held

his arm in front of her. He leaned in close to whisper in her ear. Her pulse was visible in her neck.

"It's going to be okay. Call the police. I'm going to try to pen him with the dogs. Once I have him, take Naomi and Jess inside and lock the doors." She nodded. Tears trembled on her lashes. He knew her instinct was to run to her sister. "It's going to be okay."

Phone in hand, she hit 911.

He took a deep breath and poised for an attack. He spun around the corner, rushing the man and slamming his body into the side of the car. The force of the contact broke his hold on Naomi.

Lexy came in from the other side and grabbed her sister, pulling her away from her surprised ex. The idiot had a gun in the waistband of his jeans. Damian pulled it out, released the cartridge and tossed the gun.

Naomi was crying. Lexy had the car between the men and them. She opened the back door and removed a crying Jess.

Now that the surprise was wearing off, Steve struggled to get free.

"Go." Damian kept his attention fully on the man he had pinned against the car. "You called the police?"

"Yes." She pulled her sister away. "I texted Belle and Xavier too."

"Go inside and lock the door." He motioned for Gretel to go with them.

"Naomi, baby," Steve whined. "I didn't want to hurt you. I just need to talk to you." He tried swinging his arm out, but Damian kept him pinned facedown against the car. A deep growl drew his attention. Hansel stood at attention, ready to attack.

"Be still or I'll let him have you."

"I just needed to explain." His voice was muffled but still defiant.

"She made it clear she didn't want to talk." Damian shoved his arm harder into the back of Steve's neck. Hearing Naomi's cries and seeing the red mark on her face made him want to do so much more than hold the creep in place for the police.

Rage and anger boiled inside Damian, but he took a deep breath and refused to let the emotions control him. Instead, he muttered, "You'd better start hoping the police get here soon."

The man kept whining and making excuses. Damian wasn't sure how long they'd stood there, but his leg was going stiff. Still, he didn't feel any pain, just rage. This man had come onto his property and hurt someone he cared about.

He might have growled when Lexy rejoined them. She picked up the now-unloaded gun. "Xavier's here."

A large vehicle came around the cabin. His brother stepped out. He came up next to Damian and pulled Steve's other arm behind him. "You can stand down, Damian."

"No."

"I just wanted to tell her that I'm sorry. If she comes with me everything will be fine. She's in danger but I can—" Steve coughed as Damian applied more pressure.

Lexy came closer.

Damian glared at her. "You need to be somewhere safe, far away from this bag of dirt."

She glared back. "He tried to kidnap my sister, and now he says she's in danger." She leaned down to make eye contact with Steve, still stretched over the hood of the car. "What do you mean, she's in danger?"

"Those guys. I owe them money. I had something that belonged to them. I was… I was supposed to sell it. I thought it'd be easy money. Then I thought she stole it from me, and I didn't have the stuff or the money to give them. I didn't know what to do." He sounded as if he was about to cry.

Xavier snarled. "So you ran and left Naomi and Jessie exposed?"

He nodded as he tried to suck in air. "I didn't mean—"

"Yeah. We get it. You didn't mean for her to get hurt. Are they still after her?"

"That— That's why I needed to talk to her." He looked at Lexy. "She wouldn't answer my calls or texts. What else was I supposed to do?"

Damian stepped back and let Xavier take over. His hand went into a fist, but he kept it at his side. "Be a man and face the problem you created."

More cars arrived out front.

The sheriff joined them. Steve had ignored the restraining order and assaulted her with a gun he didn't even have a license for. After a few more questions, an officer read him his rights and led him to the sheriff's car in handcuffs. The sheriff turned to them once more. "Officer Sanchez will need statements from each of you." With a reassuring smile he nodded and followed the other officer to the sheriff's SUV.

Damian turned to Lexy. "Are you okay? Naomi? Why didn't you stay inside?"

"We're fine. Belle's inside with Naomi. I had to know what kind of danger my sister was in because of him.

You and Xavier had him secured. And I wanted to make sure you were okay and the gun was out of the way."

He bit down on his back teeth, his heart still racing. Lexy had come back to protect Naomi and him.

She looked down, then gasped. "Oh, no." She covered her mouth. "My mother's sand dollar."

He looked down at their feet. The sand dollar that always hung from her rearview mirror in the dirt, broken into tiny fragments. He gently to pick up the pieces.

Tears filled her eyes as she touched the shattered sand dollar that laid in his rough hands. "It's destroyed."

"I'm sorry." The words were useless, but it was all he had.

Her breathing became rough. "It's just an object. Naomi and Jess are safe." Another sob escaped.

Not knowing what else to do, he slipped the broken sand dollar into his pocket of his jacket and pulled her in next to him.

Xavier came back from talking with the police. "Everything okay?"

Lexy stepped away and wiped her face. She gave Xavier a smile. "Just the shock, now that everyone is safe."

He nodded and patted Damian on the shoulder. "You caught the bad guy. You're a hero. Again."

Damian shook his head. No, he wasn't a hero. "I'll be in the barn if anyone needs me."

"I'll go with you." Lexy offered, reaching out to him.

Moving out of her reach, he shook his head. "No. Stay." He hated the hurt in her eyes. The hurt he put there. The acid of anger was still turning his stomach. He turned away from them. He kept a gentle grip on the shards of her sand dollar.

Xavier followed. Of course he did.

"Damian. Don't shut her out."

Not saying a word, Damian looked him in the eye and closed the barn door. That should be a clear enough message even for his big brother.

Anger still boiled inside his gut and head. He leaned against the wall and buried his fingers in his hair.

Steve said he didn't mean to hurt her. In the early days, his father had done the same, repeatedly promising that he'd do better. His mother's face and arms had proved otherwise.

Eventually, his dad had stopped apologizing and begging for forgiveness. Instead, he'd blamed her, the kids and the ranch. His anger was everyone else's fault.

Damian leaned against the wall and tipped his head back. Today had been a great day of epiphanies. He'd enjoyed going to church, sitting with Lexy and his family. It felt right. Like he was where he was supposed to be. But then he'd lost that calm—and it hadn't taken long, either, for the rage and anger to take over.

When he pinned Steve down to that car, he felt his father. He felt that rage.

God, I want to trust You. I want to face my fears and tell Lexy I love her. But I can't trust myself.

Had God put Steve in his path to remind him how close he was to being that monster?

Chapter Fourteen

"Are you sure about this?" Lexy stood in his kitchen, making a fresh bottle for Jess. "I can stay and let Naomi go with the women. She's been working hard at her new job and now with all of Steve's stupid drama she deserves—"

"I got this." They'd been avoiding each other for the last five days, since he'd walked away from her. It was for her protection.

He bounced the baby on his thigh, ignoring Lexy as she moved around in his space. "Your aunt doesn't trust me to take care of you for a few hours. Can you believe that?" Jess grinned.

If he could really ignore her, that would be great, but not making eye contact would hopefully keep his feelings hidden.

Being around her made him hyperaware of his feelings for her. Then again, when he was alone, all he did was come up with plans to be around her while she was still on the ranch. He was so messed up.

His resolution to keep his distance was not working out so well. Hunter was back this week, so she didn't need him to dive with her. There had been no reason to seek her out. Until Naomi asked him to babysit.

"Damian." Her voice was pitched higher than normal. "That's not it. I just—"

"I'm ready!" Naomi rushed through his door. He smiled that she felt comfortable enough to rush in without knocking. "Sorry. I couldn't decide how to wear my hair. Then I couldn't find my other shoe. This is going to be so much fun." She came over and kissed Jess on the cheek. "Bye, sweet girl. Mama will be home soon."

With a twirl, she went back to the door. "I've never been invited to a girls' night out before." She paused, then looked back at Lexy. "What's wrong?"

"Nothing," Lexy tried to claim.

Damian snorted. "She's having separation anxiety. That or she doesn't trust me. Not sure which one it is."

"I was thinking of staying here with Jess." Their words overlapped.

Naomi's shoulders slumped and the shine in her face dimmed. "If you don't go, I'm not going either. Damian is good with Jessie. She loves him." The baby girl kicked out her legs and babbled in agreement.

"Oh, I didn't mean anything against Damian," Lexy stammered.

He quirked an eyebrow at her but didn't say anything.

Lexy grabbed her purse. "Why are you just standing there? Unless *you* want to stay with Dami—"

Naomi grabbed her arm. "Nope. Let's go."

Lexy stopped again. "We're driving into town with Belle. Please call if you need anything or—"

Naomi grabbed her arm and pulled. "I'm the mom. He'll call me if there's a problem."

"Go," Damian ordered.

The door closed behind them. "Mommy and Tía Lexy are silly, aren't they, Jess?" The baby laughed back at him. His phone vibrated on the other side of the room. It was Xavier. Frowning, he sat Jess on her blanket and answered.

"What's wrong?"

"Nothing." Xavier laughed. "Maybe. We have ten kids and three adult males. But we've got it covered. With the ladies heading to town, we decided to gather the troops at the ranch house. Naomi said you had Jessie, so I thought I'd invite you over, now that you've become kid friendly. Besides, you haven't met your newest nephew yet. You aren't avoiding them, are you? A bleary-eyed Elijah has Daniel waiting for you."

A month ago, he would have said no. But he also wouldn't have been babysitting. "Yeah. I'll join y'all. Someone needs to keep an eye on you guys. I think they left the car seat on the porch."

"If not, let us know. Car seats are not a problem around here. Need any help?"

"Nope."

The three oldest girls were on the porch waiting. As soon as he had the truck in Park, they had the door open, talking to the dogs as they got Jess out of her car seat.

"Hi, Tío Damian. You get to see Daniel. He's so cute. This is going to be fun. We have pizza from town."

The girls talked over each other, speaking so quickly he wasn't sure who said what.

He and the dogs followed them into the house. Gretel stayed close to Jessie. In the house, pizza boxes and kids seemed to be all over the place. A tent made of sheets took up most of the dining room. Quinn was the first to see him. "There you are. Welcome to the house of controlled chaos."

Xavier caught him in a bear hug and patted him on the shoulder. "Grab some pizza. The older kids have set up an obstacle course outside."

"Like when we were kids?"

"They might be even more competitive than we were. Rosie's determined to beat the older girls." Elijah joined them, a tiny baby sleeping in one arm and a slice of pizza in the other.

"Is that pineapple?" Damian asked in horror.

"Nope. This is Daniel James De La Rosa. Your newest and best nephew." Elijah ignored the jab at his favorite pizza and showed off his bundle. "Want to hold him?" Without waiting for a reply, he slipped the baby into his cousin's arm.

Damian looked at the thick dark hair and tiny features. "He's so little."

"Nah. He's bigger than he was a month ago. He's almost ten pounds." Elijah touched his cheek as the gray-green eyes fluttered open. "He is pretty amazing, isn't he?"

Not knowing what else to say, Damian nodded. He couldn't imagine finding out about a daughter when she was five. Xavier and Quinn had moved on to kid corralling. He checked to see where the girls had taken Jess. She was sitting under one of the tents with the triplets, who were giving her toys.

Elijah took his son back and cradled him in his arms, swaying gently back and forth.

Gretel gave a low bark. Jessie was fussing and, when she made eye contact with him, she lifted her arms.

One of the three-year-old triplets tried to give her his blanket.

Damian crossed the room and picked her up. "What is it, baby girl? It's a little busier here than at home, isn't it?" She started sucking her thumb. The little guy handed him the blanket. "Thank you." The boy looked just like Xavier.

"She has you trained already." Elijah chuckled.

Damian frowned at him. "I'm not going to let her cry."

"Yeah. I find it interesting that we're all drawn to kids. Frank didn't want anything to do with us. If we needed something, we didn't go to him."

"He didn't like people in general, but he actively hated kids."

"Why do you think we're all so different from him? He raised us."

The girls ran in, Cassie leading the way. "Daddy said to get everyone outside. We want to run the course."

Elijah went to the tent. "Come on, Oliver. We're all going outside."

"No." The voice came from deep inside the tent. He was the one who had been helping Jessie.

Damian shifted Jessie so he could lift the top of the tent. "Hey, big guy. Baby Jess wants to go out to see what's going on, but she wants you to come with us. Do you know where the others are?"

Oliver crawled out and led them to the back porch. Elijah came up beside him. "I'm truly impressed. Oliver can be difficult. You were made to be a father."

Damian snorted. "I'm not anywhere close to being father material." He sat on the outdoor sofa on the back porch. Jess cuddled closer, half-asleep on his shoulder.

Oliver climbed up and scooted next to him, holding a stuffed toy close as he watched the others running around in the backyard.

Elijah raised a brow. "Are you serious? Take a minute to look at yourself." He settled in the rocking chair.

Damian ignored him. "If you want to join them, you can put Daniel in that playpen thing over there, and I'll watch him."

"Right, because you hate kids." Elijah chuckled. "I'm good. I have a feeling he's going to be too big for me to hold before I'm ready anyway. I missed all this with Rosie. It's my own fault, but it's still hard to think about. Don't want to miss a minute with this one."

Baby Jess fought sleep. The games finished up and the little ones were all starting to drag, so Xavier and Quinn herded them inside.

It was *Princess Warrior* movie night. The kids reminded Damian of a big litter of puppies, all snuggled together on a big quilt in a mess of pillows and stuffed toys.

Jess smiled and reached her small hand up to touch his face. Her sigh was deep and peaceful as she drifted off to sleep. She completely trusted him to keep her safe. Suddenly, his heart was too big for his chest.

Xavier was on the floor with the kids. Elijah looked to be dozing off with his baby sound asleep on his chest.

They had broken Frank's legacy. But the real question was: Could he?

He kept telling himself that he didn't want to hold Lexy back or get in the way of her dreams, but maybe he was just a coward. Maybe he'd been pretending to be noble in letting her go for her sake when in fact it was his own lack of faith.

* * *

With arms full of bags from local shops, boas around their necks and tiaras on their heads, they didn't look like the same group of women who had left a few hours ago. Lexy had never enjoyed a night out so much before. Watching her sister laugh and joke with their new friends made her realize how isolated they had become since their mother's illness and death.

Stepping into the large family room of the main ranch house, all the women stopped. As one they made that our-hearts-are-melting sound when they saw the kids and dads cuddled on the floor. Jazz and Selena took pictures.

Jazz took a close-up of her son and husband sound asleep on the sofa before lifting the baby off his chest. Still half asleep, Elijah shot straight up and grabbed for Daniel. Blinking then, he looked Jazz up and down and grinned. "You look like you had fun."

"We had a blast. They made a scavenger hunt out of Main Street so we had to visit each store."

Belle laughed and tossed the end of her purple boa back around her neck. "I've never had so much fun shopping."

Quinn sat up, resting his arm on his bent knee. "What? You hate shopping."

"No one ever made it a competition before. And with tiaras." She sat in the rocking chair close to her husband. Their two youngest climbed into her lap.

Selena laughed as she sat down next to Xavier and their triplets. "It should go without saying that Belle won the scavenger hunt."

Lexy adjusted her tiara, her heart fluttering as the couples reconnected. She'd never been around so many couples in harmony with each other. "Thank you so much for inviting us."

In a tall overstuffed chair, Damian held Jess against his shoulder. Snuggled close to him, she was sound asleep. He gave her his half-hearted grin, like he was afraid of showing too much happiness.

An image of him holding their nonexistent child emerged in her mind. Why was there a longing for something that would never happen? He'd made it clear there would be no relationship—let alone children—in their future.

He had to see what a wonderful parent and partner he'd make.

Naomi slung Jessie's backpack over her shoulder and reached for her daughter. "I don't think I've ever enjoyed a night out like I did this one."

After saying goodnight to everyone, he followed them out. Keeping his hand on Lexy's back, he stayed close to her.

Naomi was still bubbling. "How was Jess? Did she enjoy being around so many kids?"

"The girls spoiled her, then she hung out with Oliver. He's the quiet one of the triplets. When she got tired of it all, she asked me to pick her up. Held her little arms in the air and waited for me to do as she wanted." His chuckle was low and warm. "It's pretty astounding when they trust you like that."

Lexy smiled and leaned into him for a brief moment. "It is." She could so clearly see the nurturing man behind the cold and indifferent facade. Why couldn't he?

Once they had the car seat transferred and Jess secured, Lexy took Damian's hand, halting his movement toward the truck.

Surprised, he looked at her. "What is it?"

"Can we talk?" For days, she hadn't been able to get him out of her head. They had crossed some barriers, but then he had pulled back again. She wanted him back in her life, but she was at a loss as to how to do that.

"Good idea!" Naomi nearly yelled from the opposite side of the car. "She'll ride with you. Jess and I are going straight to bed. Take as much time as you need." She gave them a huge smile and a wave, then slid behind the steering wheel.

"Hey!" Lexy protested, staring after her car as Naomi drove off without her.

Damian snorted. "You're stuck with me."

This wasn't what she'd had in mind when she'd asked him to talk. "I meant in the morning over coffee." She wasn't sure she should be alone with Damian. He had her on a roller coaster of emotions and she didn't like it. She couldn't trust herself around him.

"Looks like it's going to be now." Taking her hand seemed so natural to him as he guided her to his truck.

She told herself to pull her hand out of his, but she didn't listen. She loved his warmth.

The silence was heavy as the truck moved slowly over the newly graded dirt road. The barn came into view. It was so much like the night she had first arrived with Naomi and Jess.

They crossed the cattle guard. "We're here, and you haven't done any talking."

"I know." She had his full attention, so what did she do now? Blurting "I love you" didn't seem right.

He sighed. "Come inside the barn."

"I'm feeling like a fly talking to a spider."

He laughed. "No webs. I promise."

"Do you think we could walk to your favorite spot? Is it too dark?"

"I've walked it at nigh as much as during the day." He grinned at her then came around to her side of the truck. His hand gently took hers, again. "Okay, so we're going for a silent walk. I like your kind of talking."

He stopped to get flashlights, then they headed out of the barn toward the ocean. The dogs on either side of them. All the words and emotions swirled in her head. Her heart started pounding.

The moon hung heavy and low over the horizon, illuminating the tall grasses that surrounded the narrow path. "We could turn off the flashlights and enjoy the night sky," she suggested.

"They're more to scare off creatures than to light our way."

She glanced around the path they were following. Grasses rustled and katydids chirped. What else was hiding in the dark?

"You said you wanted to talk." His voice was low and calm. "Why all the middle-of-the-night silence?"

They arrived at the crest overlooking the Gulf. She looked up and the view stole her breath. The full moon looked enormous hovering over the water. Its bright reflection danced on the waves. The quiet held so many sounds of nature. Some she could make out; with others, she had no clue. "How can someone experience this and not see the majestic nature of God?"

"Some people prefer to be blind to what is right in front of them." He took off his hoodie and spread it on the ground, then used Hansel to balance himself as he lowered his body. "Sit."

"It's cold. You should be wearing your hoodie."

"I'm fine." Easing down next to him, Lexy tried to keep her distance.

"Now can you tell me why we came all the way up here to have a talk?"

"The other day I asked what you would do if I stayed. I can't get rid of that idea." She took a deep breath and held it for a count of five, then let it out again. How did she say this?

"Damian. I love you."

There, that was how. Holding still, she kept her eyes on the full moon.

God, please hold my tongue. Let him process that before I go into a nervous rant.

"Don't say that."

"Why is it so wrong?"

"Stop, Lexy. We'd never work."

"I shouldn't have said anything. How many times do you have to tell me, right? You've made it clear you're not interested. I get it. You don't see a future with someone like me."

"Someone like you? What does that even mean?" He turned from the sky to face her head-on. "Any man would love to have someone like you by his side."

She snorted. "I haven't dated much, but I've dated enough to know that I'm bossy, I talk too much about my family, I don't watch TV or movies, I'm clueless about pop culture, blunt, and go on and on about the ocean and my work. And those are just a few of the reasons I never get a second date."

"I love all those things about you. Well, maybe not the bossy part." He looked at her and grinned. His hand went to her hair. "Your tiara has slipped."

The tiara from their lady's night out. She's forgotten it was there.

He leaned in so close that she could smell hints of his wintermint gum, and all thought of the sparkly head piece vanished.

"But, Lexy, I'd take bossy over someone that never has their own opinions. You listen to others and change course when needed. There are a lot of traits worse than being bossy. Anyway, Belle is bossy, and I just ignore her when she tells me something, I don't want to hear."

She laughed. "Okay, so you're unusual among the men I've met and dated. But if I'm so perfect, then why do you keep pushing me away? I don't understand. I thought we had really connected. I can't do this back-and-forth thing. Either you want to have a relationship with me, or you don't. Which is it?"

Pulling away, he rested on his arm. "Every time I start thinking we could make it work, I get a reality check. I'm sorry about the mixed messages. It's unfair of me."

She reached for him, pulling them closer together. "Damian—"

"You don't really know me. No one does. You want to know why I stay away from town and my family? Guilt." He pressed his lips together and visibly swallowed. "I killed my father."

"No. I don't believe that."

With only an inch between them, he stared into her eyes. "Because you don't know me." Each word slow and harsh.

She wanted to yell at him that she did, and that she wouldn't believe for a minute he could kill if it wasn't self-defense. His face was stone-cold then he turned his face to the Gulf. The soft glow of the moon highlighted his hard profile. Her heart slammed against her chest.

Biting her lips, she held back the words. She gave him the time and space to explain. She understood wanting to be seen as a person, not just as a tragedy.

He was so much more, and it broke her heart that he didn't see the gifts he had. Gifts a broken world needed.

Finally, she leaned in closer, giving him her warmth, a silent encouragement to continue. She rested her head on his shoulder and waited. His heart was beating fast.

"I saw him that morning." His voice was lower than usual. "At the main barn. He could hardly sit in the saddle. I'm not sure how he mounted. When I said he was too drunk to ride, he told me he wasn't going to listen to a useless one-armed, one-legged cowboy who was too stupid to avoid a bomb."

She gasped. His jaw popped as it flexed.

"Damian." Her throat was so tight it hurt to whisper his name.

He shook his head. "I was so angry. I told him to go ahead and die. I was finished with him. Then I left, not once looking back or checking on him."

She flattened her hand against his chest. Tears fell, but she knew he would see them only as pity.

"I just walked away. I knew someone should go with him. I should have followed or at least warned Belle. But I didn't do anything. The next morning, she came out to my place to ask if I'd seen him. He never returned. I found his horse grazing in the four-fifty. He was on the ground. Already gone."

"Damian, that's horrible, but no one blames you." She longed to wrap her arms around him, but just tightened her grip on his bicep. "Why do you?"

"I should have gone with him. Done something. But I was angry and so tired of his insults. I just let him die. I haven't told anyone that I saw him that morning."

Lexy sat up and gently turned his face to her, until they were eye to eye. "It wouldn't matter if they knew. He made the choices that led to his death. He is the only one responsible. Not you. I know they would all agree."

He closed his eyes. The tears that slipped past his lashes tore at her heart. Cupping his face, she leaned and rested her forehead on his. Their tears dropped between them, mixing.

"Listen to me, Damian. You are a good man. A man who took the time to help a teenage boy find the confidence to ask his girl to dance. Selfish men don't do that."

"He has as much of a right to dance as anyone else." His voice was edged with bitterness. "Belle never got to go to her dance, because I didn't protect her." He pulled away. His jaw was rock hard.

Swallowing a sob, she brought her other hand to his face. "You carry so much guilt for things you had no control over."

"There's a darkness inside me that I can't risk letting out. Frank broke me, Lexy. You don't understand. I don't think there's enough heart in me to give to anyone. He beat at it until nothing was left. That's the hardest thing to live with. You and Naomi have brought all my early Christmas memories to the surface. How or when did my father become that monster?"

"There could be so many reasons and none of them have to do with you. He drank. That's a huge one. Unchecked substance abuse takes control of a person."

He shook his head. "The bottom line is we don't

know. I can't put the people I care about at risk. I won't put you at risk."

"You care about me?"

He laughed. "Out of everything I said, that's what you got?"

"That's kind of a big deal. What do we do if I care about—"

"Nothing." The word was hard and fast. "Because that's the point I'm trying to make. My mother gave my father everything. And he broke her." He practically growled the words.

"Damian."

"I don't want the darkness in me to hurt you. I'd never forgive myself."

"Everyone's broken. That's why we turn ourselves over to God." Tears threatened again. He was hurting so much. "There's darkness we're all born with—we either hide it or give it over to God. Some don't, and you can see it in their actions. Steve, your father. Naomi's father." She hit her chest with an open palm. "I want to give up sometimes or lash out at people, but I don't."

He stood using Hansel. "I had Steve pinned against the car. I wanted to…" His fingers flexed in and out of a fist.

She stood. "But you didn't. He said he didn't want to hurt Naomi, but he did. There's a huge difference. Don't you see that?"

He stood rigid as he looked over the ocean, the moon's light creating a silhouette of his ridged form. "You have big dreams that you've worked hard to achieve. I'm not going to be someone you regret. I'm not worth it. I don't have enough to give you."

He turned on his flashlight and went to the path that would take them back to the cabins.

He was right, she did have big dreams. But what if he was part of those dreams now?

Chapter Fifteen

Damian stretched his arm behind his head. Everyone was in town celebrating the big Christmas festival Selena had started last year. His brother's wife had tried to get him involved…as if there was hope for him. The cabin next door was dark and quiet. He'd have to get used to that again.

Naomi had come over yesterday to tell him that the passports had arrived. They'd be leaving the first week of January.

When he'd told her he was happy for her, she'd seemed disappointed. Disappointment. That's what he gave people.

He glanced at the Bible that had become his early morning and after-dinner routine. If he truly wanted to stop disappointing the people he loved, he was going to have to get his act together. Through God, he had the power to change.

Picking up the book, he turned to a marked page in Corinthians. A smile pulled on his lips as he read. *For we walk by faith and not by sight.*

The words had a whole new meaning for him—he

knew what it meant to have to learn to walk all over again. Physically, yes, but now spiritually too. Something inside had held him when he fell. His mother had told him that God would never abandon him, even when others did. And she'd been right.

God had been there the whole time, through every step and stumble. He read the rest of the passage. He paused at the last line and then reread it: *For we must all appear before the judgment seat of Christ; that everyone may receive the things done in his body, according to that he hath done, whether it be good or bad.*

He sat back and looked to the sky. Stars were making their appearance as the last of the sun's light gave way to night. He would be held accountable for his choices. The good and the bad. Him, no one else.

God had gotten him through the nightmare of his childhood and the loss of his limbs, so why was he doubting Him now?

Belle had told him that it had taken more than just admitting that she loved Quinn. She'd had to let down her guard and allow Quinn to love her too.

How would he be judged by God if he sent Lexy away when God had brought her to Diamondback? Not because of him, but for her?

God did everything with purpose. He had to have brought Lexy into his life for a reason. Did she need him as much as he needed her? Was he causing more damage by turning his back on her? What if he opened his arms?

He knew that his future without her was much dimmer. Was it the same for her?

With a new urgency in his heart, he stood. "Hansel, we're going to town."

* * *

Lexy stood in the middle of the most joyous celebration she had ever been to. Lights and music—they'd even managed to produce snow in seventy-five-degree weather. It was fake, but the kids and adults were loving it.

Naomi bumped her. "Hey, you okay?"

With a nod and a smile, she tried to look happy. "This is amazing."

"It is. I'm taking Jess to the cookie-decorating booth. Want to come?"

"No, I'm good. I might head home."

"What? What's wrong?" Naomi checked Jess in the stroller.

"Nothing. It's just been a long day and the dive this morning was a tough one."

Her sister narrowed her eyes. "You miss Damian. Go talk to him."

"I did. He walked away."

She took Lexy's hand. "He's missing you too. I know he is. The other day he looked so sad."

"He's always sad."

"That's not true. Go talk to him. You've never liked big crowds anyway. I'll catch a ride home with Belle." Naomi kissed her cheek, then headed off to the booths.

In the plaza, families took turns posing for pictures in an antique red sleigh. She'd love to have one picture of her and Damian. She had taken a bunch of him while they were diving and she had some of him riding, but none of them together.

Belle stopped beside her. "You look way too sad to be at Christmas by the Sea. What's going on? Does it have to do with a certain De La Rosa male we both know and love?"

"Am I so obvious?"

"Only to someone who's fought that battle herself. You need to talk to him."

Lexy rolled her eyes. "Have you tried talking to him? I told him about how I feel. He said it wasn't enough."

Belle played with the edge of her jacket. "I promised myself I wouldn't interfere with other people's lives, but I know he loves you. Once, when I was about to shut the door on Quinn forever, Damian was there to save me from myself. Self-doubts were the only thing truly stopping me from taking a risk on love."

She looked across the street where Quinn was making ornaments with all five of their children. A secret smile that held an ocean's worth of love softened her face. "He was right."

As she turned to face Lexy, the softness vanished, and determination replaced it. "It's time for me to return the favor, but he's the most stubborn of all the hardheaded De La Rosas and won't listen to me. So, I'm going to tell you. He loves you so much it's terrifying him. I know that's not an excuse, but he's worth the fight. He's gotten too comfortable living out in his cabin without people. It's not what he really wants or needs, but it's easy. I was hoping you would be the one to fight for him."

Lexy sighed. Watching the families of Port Del Mar enjoying the Christmas festivities made her long to be with Damian. She wanted what Belle had with Quinn. "I can't be in this fight alone, Belle. He has to want it too."

Belle took her hand. "I know, and that's what hurts me the most, because I know he wants it. You didn't know him before. The changes in him since you sneaked into his barn are unbelievable. Everyone sees them."

She leaned forward, tears in the eyes that looked so much like Damian's. "He's coming to church and talking to people." Belle pulled Lexy closer and hugged her. "He did it for you."

Lexy had already been sad thinking about him isolated in his cabin. He didn't like big crowds, but that didn't mean he wanted to be alone. "I was thinking of taking some of the decorated Christmas cookies to him."

"Do it. Everything else can be figured out later."

"Okay. Taking Naomi and Jessie home isn't a problem for you?"

"Of course not. You're family." She winked, then went to join her husband and kids.

Jogging across the street, Lexy took one of the cookies her sister and niece had decorated, then with a hug goodbye went to her car. With a deep breath she pointed her car toward the ranch.

She didn't want to spend Christmas without Damian. She didn't want to spend the rest of her life without him.

Just as she cleared town, she spotted a familiar truck coming in. Damian was driving into town. Her heart picked up its pace. She slowed to make sure it was him. He slowed, too, and was looking at her. After they passed, he stopped his truck and made a U-turn.

Pulling over to the shoulder, she got out of her car. He pulled up and parked behind her. She was having a hard time breathing. Was something wrong? Why would he be here?

She climbed out and held on to the frame of her door. He walked toward her, Hansel by his side. He wore the lose running pants he preferred when not at the barn. She smiled. His cowboy hat was in its place.

"Lexy. Is everything okay?" He scanned her car with concern. "Where're Naomi and Jess?"

"They were having too much fun to leave, but I was ready to come home. I was feeling lonely." She closed the space between them.

"Lonely? You were in town with everyone." Brushing the fake snow off her shoulder, he looked confused.

"The person I was missing wasn't there." She rolled her bottom lip between her teeth.

The space between his eyes formed a deep V. "Who?"

She tipped her head and looked at him. She was sure her heart was in her eyes. Not knowing how to tell him, she stepped closer and brushed her lips against his. "You."

His hand came up and cupped the back of her neck. Leaning into her, he went deeper with the kiss, like a man getting his first drink of water after working all day in the hot Texas sun.

"In my dreams, I have two arms to wrap around you. What if I'm not enough?"

"You are everything I need and more."

He stepped back, but his hand slid down her arm to capture her hand. "You were coming back to the cabins for me?"

"I was. I have a cookie for you." Her chest was so tight it hurt.

"A cookie?" He raised one brow and tilted head.

"Yes, but…" She swallowed. "I wanted to talk to you. I know you have doubts, but I think we have something special. Our love can be bigger than our fears and doubts. If we walk away without trying, that might be our greatest regret."

She touched his face. "On the other hand, giving

love a chance might be the bravest thing either of us has done. We have to try." She narrowed her eyes. "Wait. You were driving into town. Why?"

He smiled then looked up to the sky. Twisting his lips to the side, he nodded. "I was. Last weekend, before Steve showed up, Belle said a few things that have been rolling around in my head. I had to work through them, but there are two things I know for sure. One, I love you. Two, I need to trust God if I'm going to live the life He has planned for me. The two together equal me trusting my love for you."

"You were coming to town for me?" Her eyes burned. She had so much to say, but if she spoke, she'd lose the last piece of control. She squeezed his hand.

He pressed a kiss to the corner of her eye. "I'm a slow processor. If you allow me to love you, I promise you will have everything of me." He scanned the area. "We should get off the road. Do you want to go to town or the cabins?"

"You'd go with me?"

"I'd go anywhere with you, even Argentina. I'm not letting you give up on your dreams and passions."

"Really? You'd travel with me? What about the horses?"

He laughed. "I can't be gone for long periods of time, but I'm sure Belle and Elijah could handle the horses a week here and there. I've been thinking about this all week. I'm also good at being by myself, so I don't need you glued to me. We can make this work. Can we give it a try?"

"Yes. Damian, you already have my heart, I love you so much. You've become a big part of my dreams." She thought about taking him to the antique sleigh for a photo, but that could wait. "Let's go to the cabin and enjoy our Christmas lights."

He kissed her. "I'll meet you on my porch." They stood there a little longer, neither wanting to be the first to let go.

She lifted his hand to her lips and gently bit his thumb, then laughed at his scowl. Turning, she went to her car and pulled out onto the road.

He'd been on his way into town to get her. She laughed. There was a superb chance that her side trip to Port Del Mar had changed her life forever in a way she would never have dreamed.

Not worried about hiding, she parked in front of his porch and ran up the steps. She flipped his Christmas lights on and sat in one of the rocking chairs to wait for him.

It didn't take long for him to pull his truck up next to her car. He stood in front of his truck and just stared at her.

"What are you doing?"

"I'm looking at every dream I never even knew I had coming true."

She smiled and stood. "A Christmas gift God knew we needed before we did."

He held out his hand. "Join me in the barn. There's something I want to give you."

Without a word, she went down the steps and slipped her hand into his. In the barn, he told her to wait as he went into the tack room. Hansel sat with her.

He came back with a beautiful handcrafted box the size of a paperback book. "I was going to give you this for Christmas, but I don't want to wait." He handed it to her. "Merry Christmas."

The rich wood was cut with an intricate inlay of the nativity scene. She traced the box with her fingertips. "This is beautiful. The babe in the manger."

"It was made by a local artist. But the gift is inside."

She looked up at him. "There's more?"

"Open it."

He was either going to laugh or be sick, she couldn't tell which. She flipped the little brass latch up and opened the lid. Tears sprang to her eyes. "Oh, Damian."

On a bed of black velvet lay a silver chain with two charms. A detailed silver sand dollar and a glass teardrop containing pieces of a real one. She looked up at him, her vision blurred. "It's the one my mother found on our walk."

He nodded and reached over to turn the silver charm over. "You'll never walk alone" was engraved on the back.

The tears came harder.

"Lexy. I'm sorry. I can—"

She threw herself at him. One arm clutching the box and necklace to her chest, the other going around his neck and pulling him close. "Thank you. This is…why I love you so much. You see things no one else does."

Taking a deep breath and wiping the tears away with her sleeve, she pressed her lips to his. "Damian De La Rosa, you are the man of my heart and dreams."

He pushed the hair back from her face. "You brought me back to life and gave me a reason to dream again. "My love for you is deeper than any ocean you dive. Please stay."

"You won't be able to get rid of me now."

He leaned down and kissed her. "Merry Christmas, Lexy."

Epilogue

Lexy rested a hand on Damian's arm. He was tapping the top of the steering wheel. "Are you okay? You seem nervous. Belle said the horses were great. It's only been four days. I'm sure the ranch didn't fall apart without you."

He gave her a gruff laugh, something that never grew old.

"Damian, what's wrong?"

He shook his head. "Nothing. I don't know. Maybe everything is too right. I'm not used to this level of happy. It's kind of scary."

"Are you serious?" In the last six months, she had visited three of the foundation sites and then come home to her cabin next to Damian's. California had been her longest trip at two weeks.

He had surprised her by showing up for the last four days. The team loved him.

The ranch had become her home base, and with Quinn there, there was always work to be done locally. Damian was right. Life was as close to perfect as it could be.

Maybe she should be worried too.

She rested her head on the back of her new Jeep's headrest. Damian had wanted her to drive something made to survive the ranch.

She looked over at him. He was glancing at his watch. "Damian. If we start looking for trouble, we'll miss out on all the great moments. Like now, I can feel my stress slipping away as we drive onto the ranch. The salt air in the breeze and the sun shining bright." She closed her eyes and let the vibes of her home relax her.

She must have nodded off, because when she opened her eyes, they were in front of the barn. "Is King gone?" A moment of darkness pierced her joy. "Is that why you came out to get me?" She'd been afraid to ask if they'd found a buyer for King every time they talked. His owners had deemed him useless. "They sold him, didn't they?" She wasn't going to cry.

"Yep."

She glared at him. "Why didn't you tell me? Is he still here? I didn't get to say goodbye." Her heart was breaking. She loved that horse.

Damian ignored her and headed to the barn. *Really? Just when she'd thought she really understood him, he'd go and do something like this?* He turned and looked at her.

"Are you coming?"

She jumped out of the Jeep. "He's still here? Who bought him?" Maybe he would be close. The dogs ran from her cabin to join them. Naomi waved, then went back inside.

Walking into the barn, she saw a huge red bow with streamers hanging from King's stall. She frowned. "What's that?"

Giving the dogs his full attention, he gave her a quick smile. "Go check it out."

Heart pounding, she ran to the horse. He was standing with his saddle on. His bridle hung on the peg that usually held his halter. There was a note. "Merry Christmas. I know it's six months early, but we couldn't wait. Love you, Damian and King."

She covered her mouth with her hand and cried. From behind her, Damian wrapped his arm around her shoulders and pulled her against him. His lips were close to her ear. "You're not supposed to be crying."

"How? He's…he was so far out of my price range."

"Well, after a few months, they just wanted to move him off their roster. We made a deal and I had some money I'd put back from Saltwater Cowboys. I tend to live a low-maintenance life, so I could splurge on the girl I love."

She turned around and hugged him. "This is the best non-Christmas gift ever."

"We're not done. There's a reason he has his saddle on, other than I knew you would want to ride your new horse." Giving her a quick kiss, he walked to Rio's stall. "I have something to show you."

It didn't take long for her to realize they were heading to his favorite spot overlooking the ocean. When they reached the highest point, she saw little red flags marking out an area to the left of them.

He dismounted and came to her side. "I had Quinn's guys, environmental engineers and other people, come out and tell me where the best place would be to build a house without disturbing the wildlife." He pointed to the flags.

"That's the footprint of our new house—if you want

it. It's in the early planning stage, so you can make adjustments."

"A house?" She was so confused.

He rested his head against King's neck. "I've messed this all up." He took a deep breath and looked up at her, his hand up. "Lexy, will you join me?"

Nodding, she slid off King and took his hand. She was having a hard time breathing. Was he going to do what she thought he was about to do?

He led her into the center of the flags. "To the west we have the land and to the east we have the ocean." He slipped his hand inside the front pocket of his hoodie and pulled out a black velvet box.

Her lungs stopped working. Her gaze went from the box to his face. Was he sweating? He tried to open the box with his thumb, but his hand was shaking.

"Can I open it for you?"

With a disgruntled twist of his lips, he nodded. He held the now opened box in his palm.

"Lexy Zapata, will you do me the honor of being my bride and sharing this view for the rest of our lives?" He finally looked up at her. "The night you sneaked into my barn was the night I truly started living. Everything I have is yours, because without you it means nothing. With you, every day is Christmas."

Everything in her was numb. How could this be her life? She touched the charms she wore around her neck.

"Lexy?"

The single, simplest word was stuck in her throat. The tears ran freely, but she managed a nod. Then she nodded again to make sure she said yes.

She nodded until he took her in his arm and held her so tight that she might have stopped breathing.

Stepping back, he offered her the ring. She reached for it and held it up to the sun. "Oh, Damian." It was simple but flawless. "It's beautiful."

He took the ring from her and slipped it on her finger. "Does getting married Christmas Eve work for you?"

"That sounds perfect." Grabbing his face, she kissed him. "I love you. I love you so much. I can't believe this started with us lost and stumbling into your barn."

"You weren't lost. God knew exactly where you were. Right where you belonged."

He wrapped his arm around her waist and pulled her close as they stared out over the ocean. "Merry Christmas," he repeated. "I know it's early, but…" His eyes closed and his lips became a thin hard line as he fought back emotions.

Fighting back her own tears, she laughed and cupped his face. "A very merry Christmas to you."

Gently she pressed her lips to his and put her arms around him. This was where she belonged.

* * * * *

If you enjoyed this story, look for these other books by Jolene Navarro from Love Inspired:

Dear Reader,

First, I want to thank everyone who asked for Damian De La Rosa's story. Finding the right heroine for him wasn't easy but I hope you love Lexy Zapata as much as I do.

Damian has been whispering in my ears for a few years now. He was inspired the season I watched Noah Galloway, who has a double amputation, perform on *Dancing with the Stars*. Noah is a former US Army soldier and extreme-sports enthusiast.

Even though Damian doesn't have anything in common with Noah other than being an army man who has a double amputation, I wanted to honor and explore the human ability to adjust and modify in the face of such adversity.

I also loved the research for Lexy's job. I want to be an underwater photographer! Reefs are one of God's most remarkable creations. Sea Turtle, Inc., in South Padre Island, Texas, was an incredible source of information. There are so many organizations that are working tirelessly to protect our beaches and oceans.

God has given us so many gifts. I hope you enjoyed the journey that Damian and Lexy took to find their purpose in God and the courage to risk their hearts for true love.

Thank you,
Jolene Navarro

WE HOPE YOU ENJOYED
THIS BOOK FROM

LOVE INSPIRED
INSPIRATIONAL ROMANCE

Uplifting stories of faith, forgiveness and hope.

Fall in love with stories where faith helps guide you through life's challenges, and discover the promise of a new beginning.

6 NEW BOOKS AVAILABLE EVERY MONTH!

Get 4 FREE REWARDS!

*When a city slicker wants the same piece of land
as a small-town girl, will sparks fly between them?*

Read on for a sneak preview of
Opening Her Heart
by Deb Kastner.

What on earth?

Suddenly, a shiny red Mustang came around the curve
of the driveway at a speed far too fast for the dirt road,
and when the vehicle slammed to a stop, it nearly hit the
side of Avery's SUV.

Who drove that way, especially on unpaved mountain
roads?

The man unfolded himself from the driver's seat and
stood to his full over-six-foot height, let out a whoop of
pure pleasure and waved his black cowboy hat in the air
before combing his fingers through his thick dark hair
and settling the hat on his head.

Avery had never seen him before in her life.

It wasn't so much that they didn't have strangers
occasionally visiting Whispering Pines. Avery's own
family brought in customers from all over Colorado who
wanted the full Christmas tree–cutting experience.

So, yes, there were often strangers in town.

But this man?

He was as out of place as a blue spruce in an orange grove. And he was on land she intended to purchase—before anyone else was supposed to know about it.

Yes, he sported a cowboy hat and boots similar to those that the men around the Pines wore, but his whole getup probably cost more than Avery made in a year, and his new boots gleamed from a fresh polish.

Avery fought to withhold a grin, thinking about how quickly those shiny boots would lose their luster with all the dirt he'd raised with his foolish driving.

Served him right.

Just what was this stranger doing *here*?

"And didn't you say the cabin wasn't listed yet?" Avery said quietly. "What does this guy think he's doing here?"

"I have no idea how—" Lisa whispered back.

"Good afternoon, ladies," said the man as he tipped his hat, accompanied by a sparkle in his deep blue eyes and a grin Avery could only categorize as charismatic. He could easily have starred in a toothpaste commercial.

She had a bad feeling about this.

As the man approached, the puppy at Avery's heels started barking and straining against his lead—something he'd been in training not to do. Was he trying to protect her, to tell her this man was bad news?

Don't miss
Opening Her Heart *by Deb Kastner,*
available January 2021 wherever
Love Inspired books and ebooks are sold.

LoveInspired.com